Four Historica
in Small

Small-Town
Summer
BRIDES

Diana Lesire Brandmeyer, Pam Hillman,
Maureen Lang, Amy Lillard

BARBOUR BOOKS
An Imprint of Barbour Publishing, Inc.

The Honey Bride © 2015 by Diana Lesire Brandmeyer
The Lumberjack's Bride © 2015 by Pam Hillman
The Summer Harvest Bride © 2015 by Maureen Lang
The Wildflower Bride © 2015 by Amy Lillard

ISBN 978-1-63409-529-7

All scripture quotations are taken from the King James Version of the Bible.

This book is a work of fiction. Names, characters, places, and incidents are either products of the author's imagination or used fictitiously. Any similarity to actual people, organizations, and/or events is purely coincidental.

Published by Barbour Books, an imprint of Barbour Publishing, Inc., P.O. Box 719, Uhrichsville, Ohio 44683, www.barbourbooks.com

Our mission is to publish and distribute inspirational products offering exceptional value and biblical encouragement to the masses.

Member of the
Evangelical Christian
Publishers Association

Printed in the United States of America.

The Honey Bride

Diana Lesire Brandmeyer

Dedicated to Mike and Lisa Hoppe, my bee friends.

Chapter 1

May 1887, Trenton, Illinois

Wind-whipped water plopped, splattered, and then moistened Katie Tucker's forehead, rousing her. Something wasn't right. She'd fallen asleep with open windows, hoping for a breeze to relieve the early summer heat. Now the wind was wicked, pulsating against the bedroom panes and blowing in rain. She sat, reached for the window, and closed it with a bang.

The sky lit up once, twice. The hair on her arms stretched for heaven. *Crack.* The second story sizzled and popped. Lightning. She shivered. Was it a tornado, like the one she'd read about last month? Five people in Wabash County had died.

Papa would be yelling to go to the cellar any minute. *Please, God, not down there.* Chill-bumps raced up her arms.

Henry, her younger brother, banged against her door and called out, jarring her from the nightmare of spider webs stuck in her hair.

Had he said fire? In the house? The barn? Shaking, she fumbled for her wrapper, found it, then rushed her arms through the sleeves. Her shoes were by the back door. Henry waited at the bottom of the stairs.

"The barn's on fire. Papa's out there."

"Get a bucket! I'll get the stew pan. Where's Oma?"

"Sleeping."

"I'll wake her. Get as many things filled with water as you can." Henry's boots pounded sharply against the wood floor in time to her heart beat. She needed to wake her grandmother.

Oma met her at the doorway.

"What's the yelling about?"

"Lightning started a fire in the barn. Papa is getting out the animals. I was coming to wake you."

"I'm up. Go help. I'll be there as soon as possible."

Katie hesitated. Should she insist her grandmother stay inside?

"Go, *Schatzi*. Now."

Her grandmother's strong words urged her feet forward and she hightailed it down the stairs for her shoes. She trembled on the bench, trying to get her shaking fingers to work her laces into place. The unnatural noises from the animals made her want to run back to bed. No matter how fearful she was she couldn't. There was work to be done.

Outside, the smoke lay heavy in the air. They needed

help. The farmhand Papa hired hadn't shown up. If only they could get word to the fire department, but they were too far from town. She'd send Henry to the Gibbons'. They were the closest.

Henry worked the pump, water pouring, splashing against the bucket sides.

"Where's Papa?"

"Still in there. He got Starlight out first."

"Good. Get on her, ride to the Gibbons', and tell them we need help."

"I can help."

"We need more than the three of us. Hurry. You're faster than me."

Henry ran for the horse. Katie picked up the bucket of water Henry had filled. The handles bit into her hands as she carried it to the barn. "Papa! I have water!"

"I'm here." He grabbed the bucket and ran inside. Seconds later he was back. "Fill it again. Hurry." He coughed. "Where's Henry?"

"I sent him for help." Flames licked the inside of the dry barn wood.

"They won't make it before it's burned to the ground." Her father bent over coughing. When he was able to catch his breath he handed her his kerchief. "Wet that and bring it with the next bucket. Lady Jane is still in there."

She shuddered. Lady Jane was difficult on a good day. In a fire, who knew what the horse was capable of doing.

Unable to sleep, Pete Dent paced the Gibbons' barn, where he slept. The rhythm of the rain didn't bring its usual soothing. Storms didn't bother him, but this one did. Too soon, too dangerous, after the one last month. He stood in the open door and noticed Roy standing on the porch. He jogged across the yard and up the steps. "Thunder keeping you awake?"

"Scared Frances. Alma's taking care of her." Roy said.

Crack. The lightening startled both men.

"That was close. Sounded like it hit something." Roy ran to the edge of the porch.

Pete looked the other way, toward the Tucker place; Katie on his mind, again. He'd like to get to know her better. It had taken him a few months, but he'd managed to get her to smile at him at church anyway. Shy little thing. He'd been ready to pull up stakes and find another place to work when she'd caught his eye. Katie might be the one person to tip the scale and keep him in Trenton.

"Do you see that?" Roy pointed in the direction Pete had been staring.

"That's a bright light. Too bright. Think they got hit with that last bolt?" Pete's heart pounded. "I'm riding out. They might need help if it hit the house or barn."

"Go. I'll let Alma know and meet you."

Pete wasted no time saddling Biscuit and urging him to a gallop. As he grew closer to the Tucker's, he knew something was burning. Probably the barn with the way the flames were flicking the sky. Someone rode toward him. Katie coming for help? He slowed his horse.

"Hey, our barn's on fire. Can you help?"

"Henry, is that you?"

"Yeah, Pete. Katie told me to get you. Hurry! Papa's getting the animals out and. . . ." Henry stopped to catch his breath.

"I heard you. That's where I'm headed. Roy's behind me."

Henry turned Starlight around.

Both horses stretched into a neck-to-neck race for the Tucker barn.

When they arrived, the smoke was thick, but the bright flames licked through, illuminating the night, revealing Katie lugging a bucket. Pete dismounted and tied Biscuit to the porch railing. He ran to Katie and pried her fingers from the handle. "Fill another one and keep filling. I'll get them to the barn. Roy's on his way."

"Papa's in there! I can't get to him."

Cold sweat tickled down his back. If Mr. Tucker was still in that barn, the odds were he wasn't coming out. *Please, God, let her father be alive.* He ran inside, keeping low. "Mr. Tucker! Holler your position!" The roaring flames sucked his words into silence. He tossed the water on a bale of hay and ran out, gasping for air.

Katie waited with a pan of water. He took it and rushed back inside. He had to find her father.

Katie sat on the back steps, hugging Henry close to her. Waiting. Most of their church congregation either stood in the yard or were in the house. Katie and Henry sat alone. She couldn't talk to anyone, not even Alma.

Pete Dent had been kind, explaining how her father probably inhaled too much smoke and couldn't breathe. He'd seen it before, serving on the volunteer fire department. He told her to take Henry inside, but she couldn't. If she left these steps, it would be real. So she clung to Henry and waited.

Tears rolled down her cheeks, bringing some relief to the sting from the smoke.

Chapter 2

A few weeks later, Katie walked head down to avoid speaking with anyone on the street. She only had to collect the mail and return home, nothing more. She'd fussed about coming into town at all, but Oma insisted, saying it was time for a letter from Katie's sister.

The warm yeasty fragrance of fried dough and sugar drifted through the bakery door. The pleasurable scent slowed her steps. Those doughnuts sure smelled good. But were they enough to risk a conversation about that awful night? Her mouth watered, and she pictured the joy on Henry's face when she gave him one. Even Oma might perk up.

Guilt squeezed her heart. Would people think it wrong of her to buy something so enjoyable so soon after the fire and her father's death? Her desire burned and then settled into ash in her mouth. Maybe next time.

She took one last deep breath and then headed for the post office. She glanced at the bakery. It was almost as if Papa were with her. She could hear him laughing about her worrying about being judged by others again. She shook him away. He might be right, but he didn't have to live with the upturned noses.

Settled with her decision, she made her way into the post office.

"Miss Tucker, it's nice to see you in town again." Mr. Rutherford, the postmaster, turned to the row of wooden boxes where mail was filed. He pulled out a few envelopes and handed them to her.

"*Danke.* Thank you, sir." She glanced at the top letter. It was from Kentucky. Grandmother would be pleased to hear news from her other granddaughter. She wanted to rip open the envelope, but it wasn't addressed to her. Oma would share any news with her and Henry.

The other came from a bank in Lebanon, addressed to Papa. Why would they be sending him mail? This one she could open. Maybe Papa had an account there? That would be a blessing. They needed to rebuild the barn. She scooted through the door and smacked into Pete Dent.

"Whoa! Where's the fire?"

Her breath caught, and in a flash, she was back there at the barn the night of the storm, listening to him say those awful words about Papa. Her lips moved but no sound came forth.

Pete's face turned the color of rhubarb. "I'm sorry, Miss Tucker, that was—"

Not waiting for the rest of his apology, Katie brushed past him, stiff and broken as the charred beams that had collapsed in on themselves in her yard.

She headed for the bakery. People may talk, but her hope was that the sweet heaviness of a doughnut would fill the crater in her heart caused from Papa's death and Pete Dent's careless words. Shoulders straight, she marched inside and asked for three doughnuts.

The bank letter lay heavy on her mind. Last fall Papa said the farm was paid for, but what if he'd borrowed money? And why did he go to Lebanon when they had a bank here? Something wasn't right. She could feel it. *Weibliche* intuition, Oma would say, a woman always knows. She'd stop at Alma's on the way home. Then if the news were truly bad, she'd have someone to pray with her. Oma wasn't strong enough to handle any more formidable news. "Please, could you wrap another half-dozen?" She didn't want to arrive empty handed at the Gibbons'.

Pete was an idiot. He had been waiting to speak to Katie, and his first chance he'd reminded her of the one thing she wanted to forget. As it was, the memory of her sitting on the porch, hugging Henry that night, wouldn't leave him. He knew the shape of her heart, felt it in his own. The freshness of being alone returned, almost bringing him to his knees and would've, too, if he weren't a grown man. His mind told him it wasn't the same as what had happened to him. Yes, both her parents were now dead, but she had a home and family. That had to make a difference, didn't it?

"You here for the Gibbons' mail?" Mr. Rutherford had already turned to the boxes behind him. "Just one, this time."

"Thank you, sir." Pete took the letter, a little sad there wasn't one for him. Why would there be? He had no one. Even if he did, they didn't know how to find him, since he'd shortened his name from Dentice. A clean break from the past. He'd given up finding his brother, sure by now he'd have a home and family of his own. Probably didn't even remember his old last name.

Outside, he walked to the Ginzel Mercantile, where his loaded wagon waited. Did he need anything else? The doughnuts smelled good but Alma had promised a rhubarb pie for dessert. He'd hang on to his money. Someday he'd have enough for a farm of his own. In Trenton, he hoped, if he could find someone willing to sell.

He climbed up on the wagon seat and set the horse to moving. The feeling that it was time to move on, that he didn't belong here, snuck up on him last week. It wasn't Roy's fault he'd found a wife and now had time to work on his own farm. If Pete left this town, he'd sure miss those little girls, Elsibet and Frances. They had him thinking of settling down and having children, made him feel like this town could be his home.

Pete hadn't gone far when he spotted Katie, walking. Her shoulders were rounded as if she literally carried the death of her father on them.

She moved closer to the side of the road for him to pass. Instead, he slowed the horse, and then stopped beside her. "Miss Tucker, would you care for a ride?"

Her hat barely tipped up far enough for him to see her eyes before she looked away. "Yes, I'd—"

Pete climbed out of the wagon ready to help her board before she finished her sentence.

"Thank you. You won't have to take me far. I plan to visit Alma."

"I'll be happy to see you home, after." He glanced at her. She was studying a letter.

"Good news?"

She startled, grabbing the edge of the bench seat.

"I'm sorry. I didn't know you were lost in thought."

Katie looked at him for a second. Her blue eyes were watery. What should did he do about that? Should he ask if she was crying or offer a hanky? Maybe it was dust in her eyes? There was enough of that floating in the air.

"No. It's not."

"Not what?"

"Good news. My father took out a loan and it's due in August. I—I need to see Alma." She sniffled.

Tears then. He guessed she didn't want him to know how bad things were because she said nothing and kept her head turned.

How much had her father borrowed? Did that mean the Tuckers would have to sell the farm? It would be good for him. He could buy it and be close to the Gibbons. But where would Katie and her family live? She had a sister in Kentucky. Maybe she'd move there. And why did the thought of Katie living in another state bother him?

Katie couldn't clamber off the wagon fast enough. She was out before Pete could help her down. She wouldn't let him see her crying. If she didn't hurry into Alma's happy kitchen right now, he wouldn't see just a few tears but sobs.

She managed a quick "thank you for the ride" and bolted up the stairs and into Alma's arms. "I have to sell the farm. How am I going to tell Henry and Oma?"

Chapter 3

Katie slumped in the oak chair at Papa's desk. His scent clung to the room she'd rarely entered. It seemed he'd walk through the door any moment and catch her snooping through the drawers.

The information had to be here somewhere. Papa was meticulous about what needed to be done. He must have been the same about his financial records. So far she hadn't discovered this year's ledger. She opened a drawer and took out a stack of papers. There had to be a reason he'd borrowed money. She and Oma had discussed it last night, and they couldn't figure it out. Nothing new had been purchased, no livestock had arrived. Even the workman she thought was supposed to come hadn't appeared.

"What are you looking for?" Henry climbed into the chair in front of the desk, as if he were at home in this room where children weren't allowed.

"Papa's ledger. I need to find out how much is in the bank and what bills are due."

"The green book?"

"How do you know it's green?"

"Because it's like mine."

"Uh huh." She'd spent a lot of time teaching her brother and reading to him since he was small. She'd never taught him how to keep accounts. Probably Papa had given him an old book to play with. She pulled more papers from the drawer and set them aside.

Henry stood. "I know where it is."

The authority in his voice made him sound older. She stopped pulling papers from the drawer and gave him her full attention. "I'm listening."

"Papa kept our books together." Henry opened the glass-fronted bookcase and removed several books. Behind them were the ledgers.

"Why did he hide them?"

"Papa said valuable information shouldn't be left where it is easily found. He was teaching me how to write down expenses so I'd know how when the farm is mine."

Which it was now. That's what Papa always said, never intending Henry to be in charge at ten.

"Could I see Papa's ledger, please?"

He held it tight against his chest then handed it to her. "Katie, I'm supposed to be the man of the house, but I don't feel like one. There's so much I don't know how to do."

She saw him fighting to keep from breaking into a sob. She had been his age when he was born, and their mother died. Over time she'd become more of his mother than a sister. She set the book on the desk and pulled him into a hug. "You have some growing to do. One day you will be in charge of this house, but for now, would you let me and Oma take care of the finances?"

Breaking away, he gave her a smile. "Does that mean I can quit school?"

"No, it means you get to work hard on the farm and come inside and do your lessons at night."

"Why? All the learning I need is outside."

"No, it's not. You have to know how to figure out how much grain we need to keep for the winter, how much to sell, and what to do with the money made."

Henry's lips twisted then his forehead wrinkled. "Do I have to start today? I wanted to go fishing."

Too soon, responsibilities would weigh on his shoulders. "Bring back something for supper."

He left so fast it was as if she'd imagined him. But she hadn't. The answers to the loan sat between green covers on Papa's desk.

Pete brushed Biscuit while waiting for Roy in the barn. He needed to pull away from this family before the pain of leaving created a scar that wouldn't heal. What would it be like if he'd been adopted with his younger brother? Would they have a place of their own? Wives? Would he be an uncle? Maybe he was already. "What do you think Biscuit? Could I be some little one's Uncle Pete?"

The curry comb moved faster, followed by the brush. He'd tried to locate Billy after he'd run away from the home he had been placed in. Some home. They gave him a room in the barn, and he ate his meals on the porch. Not much different than the way Pete lived now—except for here. He was invited in to eat with a family; two little girls followed him, always talking; even Alma had been kind, showing him how to sketch. She'd bought him a book and some special pencils to practice last winter.

He'd found himself trying to capture Katie Tucker on the paper. She was a hard subject. That's what Alma called the kittens, even though they were soft as dandelion puff. They were precious but difficult to put on paper because they wouldn't stop moving. Katie didn't move a lot, but she wouldn't look at him long enough for him to study her face.

"That horse ain't going to have any hair left if you don't stop." Roy held out a piece of pie. "Alma sent this out for you. You hurt her feelings not wanting to eat with us."

Pete closed the stall door. He set the grooming tools on a shelf and then took the pie. "I'm sorry. I'll apologize later."

"Yes, you will. Can't have my Snow Angel with tears in her eyes."

"I think it's time for me to move on."

"Why would you think that? Your home is here. My girls love you, and I need you." Roy's face turned red. "Did you get a better offer? If it's a property you want or a house, I'll sell you a piece of land and help you build."

"Hear me out before you get a pitchfork." He took a bite of the pie. He considered his words with care. "I've been wanting to talk to you about leaving, but until this week I hadn't come up with the where to go."

"Why don't you start with explaining your need to leave?" Roy settled against the barn wall.

"You know it. I told you when I came to work for you that I never settle anywhere for long. I stayed as long as I have because of the girls."

"You'll break their hearts if you leave."

"Just wait, here's my idea. When I dropped Katie off at her farm last week, it wasn't hard to tell nothing's been done since the fire. The barn smoldered and died with her father, not a board has been moved. She said her father had hired someone, but he hasn't shown up."

"So you want to buy her place?" Roy straightened. "That don't seem like you, Pete, taking advantage of two women and a boy."

Pete shook his head. "No. I don't think that's what she wants. We know her father took out a loan, so she might lose the place if we—I—don't help her."

"What's your plan? She won't accept charity."

"Thought I'd tell her you sent me to get the barn built."

"How's that not charity?"

"If Alma helps, we can do this. Katie will listen to her. Tell her you two want to loan her the money to buy the lumber and you'll pay my wages—not that I'd expect that. I've got enough saved that I can work there for a while." He kicked at some loose straw. "Besides, I think Henry needs a man around the place. Help him figure out how to run it."

Roy laughed. "And his sister? Perhaps you think I haven't seen you working up the nerve to talk to her all spring."

"I wouldn't be opposed, but I don't think she approves of me, being a drifter with no family."

"I found it's best not to put thoughts into the minds of others." Roy scratched his chin. "Let me talk to Alma. See what she thinks. She won't want you staying over there at night."

"Why would that be different than the farmhand that hasn't shown up?"

"No barn. Where do you think you'd be sleeping?"

"There, that's the reason to get Alma to get Katie to accept my help. If she hires someone else, no telling what might happen to her."

Katie's trembling hand held the screen door closed as if

it could protect her from the tobacco chewing, slovenly, smelly man on her porch. "When did my father hire you?"

"Don't much matter to you, missy. He's the one I need to see." The man spat a wad of tobacco on the porch.

Katie tried to summon her voice to tell him to leave. She couldn't let this man know Papa was dead. But if Papa hired him, how would she fire him? *Please, God, don't let Henry come up from the creek.* He'd for sure spill the news.

Taking a breath, she called on God to give her courage she knew she didn't have. "What's your name?"

"W.D. Where's your papa, missy?" His gaze traveled from her feet back to her face. "You're a right pretty gal, when you look at a man."

Her legs quivered and her stomach roiled.

Chapter 4

Still full from dinner or rather Alma's gooseberry pie, Pete rode down the lane to the Tuckers' place. He'd come with Alma's blessing and the note she'd written to Katie.

His thoughts wandered to what a future would look like with her if he had something to offer. Lost in a world that seemed more of a fairy tale, he didn't notice the man on the front porch until Katie's voice broke through.

"I said you must leave."

A man Pete hadn't seen before stood close to the door, close enough that he could've been kissing Katie through the screen.

He kicked Biscuit in the side, moving him on a little faster, not enough to alarm Katie but quick enough to help if needed.

"You're late, and Father said he wouldn't take you, seein'

as you didn't even let him know you weren't coming on time."

Her voice shook. Was she mad or scared?

"I don't think your pa is even here. Why don't you let me inside to wait for him?"

"You, there. What's your business here?" Pete halted Biscuit at the bottom porch step. "Miss Tucker? Are you all right?"

"I was telling W.D. that Papa didn't want him here."

Was she okay? Had she slipped into some kind of place where people don't remember things that happened in the past? He dismounted, looped Biscuit's reins around the spindle, and climbed the stairs. He saw Katie through the screen, her hands tight on the door handle. Her eyes were wide, beautiful, and pleading. He stood taller, much taller, than she.

"Sir, I'm sorry you've come so far out of your way. Mr. Tucker hired me on last week. He couldn't wait any longer. You understand how that could be." He pointed to the barn. "With the fire, he needed help."

"Looks like you haven't started." The man backed away from the door.

"The lumber hasn't arrived. Why don't you head back to town and ask around? Might find work at the mine."

"I ain't working underground." He shuffled closer to the steps. "Guess I ain't wanted here. I'll wait in town a few days." He left the porch and mounted his horse. "You send word when that lumber comes as Mr. Tucker might need an extra hand."

"Papa won't be needing help." Katie said.

She'd found her voice. Pete almost smiled. Her hands dropped from the handle. That small sign of trust brought a feeling he couldn't name, but he knew he liked it.

The man tipped his hat. "Like I said, I'll be around." He rode off at a slow pace.

Pete moved toward the steps. He should go after him, make sure he understood not to come back.

He noticed the wet lump of tobacco on the porch and almost called the man back to clean it, but he smelled like he'd been soaking in beer. No. He'd take care of the porch. No need to give the stranger time to figure out there was no Mr. Tucker.

Katie wasn't sure what to do about Pete standing on the porch. He'd saved her, but if she invited him inside, she'd have to talk to him, because Oma was napping. She forced a smile, pushed open the door, and stared at his boots. "Thank you. I didn't know how to make him leave."

"It was smart of you not to tell him your father passed."

She risked a look to see if he meant it. Their eyes met. Heat rushed through her, like she'd never felt before. What did that mean? She felt safe and warm, very warm.

"He made a mess of your porch." He slipped a

handkerchief from his back pocket and wiped his brow. "I'll clean it."

"I'll do it. You've done enough saving me from that man. If you hadn't come—" She laced her fingers together and squeezed her palms. "Why are you here?"

"Alma sent you a letter." He reached into his shirt pocket and withdrew a piece of paper. "Why don't you sit on the swing and read it? I'm to wait for a reply."

She grasped the note. Her fingers froze against his; they were rough and calloused, a hard working man's hand, Oma would say. The kind you want in a husband. She swallowed. "Can I get you lemonade?"

"No. Go, sit. I'll take care of this mess."

She puzzled at his kindness but accepted his offer. "There's a bucket by the pump."

"Back by the porch. I remember."

Of course he'd know that. He'd been here that night. She composed herself. "That's right. I haven't forgotten what you've done for us." She spun quickly so he wouldn't see her nose turning red as tears swelled. "I'll have an answer when you're done."

She heard him sigh, followed by his boots thumping against the porch. Only then did she risk watching him walk away. He had fine broad shoulders. His dark hair needed a trim, but she had to admit Pete Dent was the first man she'd ever wanted to look at.

Settled in the swing, the motion soothed her confusion.

A letter from Alma was unusual, but a delight to the eyes. At the top, Alma had sketched a cardinal. As Katie read the sentences, her feet, fueled by agitation, pushed the swing back harder. Did her friends truly think it was a good idea to loan her money to rebuild the barn? And what about Pete being here every day? Bumping into him at the noon meal, maybe even dinner? The swing struck the house, taking her by surprise.

Water splashed across the wood. "Guess the way you're sending that swing to the moon, you aren't liking what the Gibbons are suggesting?"

She slowed the swing and smoothed the paper on her lap. "The Tuckers don't accept charity."

"I believe it's a loan."

"What if I can't pay them back?"

"Your crops are in. After the harvest you'll have what you need."

Would she? Maybe, but there was the matter of the other loan. A bee flew up from the roses and buzzed by Katie. Screaming, she shot out of the swing and crashed into Pete.

He caught her and held her tight. "Don't move. It's when you move they sting."

Katie held her breath, her worst fear and deepest shame bound in one little body. How she'd begged Papa to have hives, only to turn her back on the idea when a sting brought welts on her arm.

"It's gone." His arms dropped to his sides.

She stepped back. The sudden release from the sweet security of his arms felt worse than the sting would've. Crossing her arms over her chest, she made a decision. "Tell the Gibbons I'll accept their kind offer."

"I'll also inform them about the stranger. I think they'll agree I need to stay here, because once he gets into town, he'll find out about your father's death."

"It has to be this way. If not, how will I protect you?" Pete held his hat and rubbed the brim with his thumb.

"No. Absolutely not. You can't stay here, not in the house. Oma won't allow that, nor would I." Katie spat the words at him. "Besides, I can shoot. I'm not in danger."

The screen door squeaked. "What's this commotion? Are you all right, Katie? Where's Henry?" Oma's questions shot as fast as a rapid-repeating rifle.

"We had a man asking about work. He said Papa hired him."

"If your father hired him, why would you send him away? We need help."

"He spat on your porch, ma'am, and was talking rough to Katie. I didn't care for him."

Oma squinted toward the field. "Where's Henry?"

"Down at the creek, catching dinner." Katie moved closer to her grandmother and patted her shoulder. "I'm sure he's fine. He'll come back, wet and muddy, carrying a fish or two."

"Can't lose another person. I won't survive it." Her grandmother's face faded like a summer blossom in early fall.

"That won't happen. Mrs. Tucker, I'm coming to stay. I was telling Katie that because the barn is destroyed, I'll have to sleep in the house."

Her head jerked up. "No. I'll not have Katie's reputation soiled."

Pete's jaw tightened. Once again cast as a man without a stellar reputation, one he'd never deserved. Traveling city to city looking for his brother and a place to settle hadn't done anything for how he was viewed by others.

"What would you suggest?"

"Get that barn done so you have a place to lay your head. Until then, you'll ride back to the Gibbons'. Katie, take me inside. I feel another headache itching to make me miserable."

Katie took her grandmother's arm. "Mr. Dent, thank you for helping me. I'll put Papa's rifle by the door. I won't be unprepared next time. And please, thank Alma. We'll see you tomorrow. I'm sure Henry will be excited to have you around."

Before Katie reached the door, Pete had it open. "Do you need help getting her settled?"

She gave him a sad smile. "We'll be fine. We're three-cord strong around here. Just like the Bible says, it's harder

TTTT

TTT

ffff

TTT

TTTT

Tffff

TTT

to break when there are three bound together."

A lump formed in his throat. He wanted too much to be one of the strands. "I'll see you in the morning."

Pete rode back to the Gibbons' to pack a kit, because he was staying over, no matter what Katie and her grandmother thought. He'd seen men, worked with some, like the one on Katie's porch. They weren't to be trusted. Protecting her from a bee was a small thing, from the stranger, much bigger, but the bee had sent her into his arms. He pushed his hat back.

"Biscuit, the woman was more afraid of that little honeybee than the man. It doesn't make sense."

Chapter 5

Still trying to cool off from the weather and Mr. Dent's assertion that she'd let him stay in her house, Katie downed a glass of lemonade. She poured another for her grandmother, who had settled in the porch rocker.

"That was a lot of excitement this morning." She handed her the cold glass. "Do you think we made the right decision? What if that man comes back?"

"Then we'll scare him off." The rocker slowed. "You aren't afraid, are you? If so, we can let Mr. Dent sleep in the room next to mine. Henry can fetch him whenever he gets back."

"No. I'm fine." She still shook, but having Mr. Dent in the house caused more alarm than the stranger returning. "I'm going to look over Papa's ledger. Are you all right?"

Oma drank the last of her drink and handed Katie the empty glass. "I'm all right. I believe I'll rest here." She settled into the chair and closed her eyes.

Katie gave Oma a long look. Had Papa's death been too much for her? Not knowing what else to do, she stepped inside Papa's office.

She began going through the pages of numbers and what they were assigned to. Nothing seemed out of place. Grain, the mercantile, even fabric purchased for aprons was listed. Flipping the page, she ran her finger down the side, more of the same, except—

Twelve dollars each for ten Italian queen bees. Heartsick, she knew what the loan had been for. She'd begged Papa to let her start a colony of bees, thinking they could sell the honey and wax for a nice profit. A few days later, she'd been stung on her face. The welt was so huge and painful that Oma had slapped mud from the garden on her face. She shuddered, remembering its slimy feel.

Had the bees come and Papa started the hives? She wasn't going searching for them, even if she did feel bad about the money spent.

That night Katie lay awake. The full moon brightened her room with its kiss of light. What if the bees were still here, making honey? How did one get it from the hives without being stung? Giving up on sleep, she slid from bed and paced the floor. Her bare feet against the waxed wood barely made a sound. The house, built by her grandfather, was exceptional. He'd put a lot of time into making sure the yellow pine floors didn't squeak. And the woodwork had taken several winters. Downstairs he'd carved roses into the newels, and ivy vines up the stair balusters and on the sides of the banister. Even the bedrooms, usually plain, were created with care; the rosettes in the doorframes were all made by her grandfather.

What else had Papa bought? How could he have put them in danger of losing their home, their heritage that was to go to Henry someday? And to her. Papa had said she could live here forever if she never married.

Had he known then, when she was fifteen, that no one would want a timid wife? One subject to tears when her nerves frayed? Papa called her his delicate rose.

She hated it. She wasn't delicate, and she wasn't fancy like a rose. No, she was more like those fuzzy bees that frightened people.

When Henry married, would she still have this room? Or would a new wife want her to move to the attic? Maybe even out of the house?

She sat on the bed, her hand tracing the quilted line in her coverlet, while she looked through the open window at the rows of corn swaying with the touch of a slight breeze. The stalks weren't quite knee high but it looked like they would be by the Fourth of July.

There had to be something she could do to make sure they kept their home. She had to figure out how much money they'd need and how to get it. Her heart seized. What if it meant working in town? She fell back on the bed. "Father, please help us. I can't go near bees. I'm too scared. And I can't work in town." Her whispered plea floated through the window.

Pete adjusted his head on the bedroll. He'd rode in late and expected to be greeted at the door with a gun barrel pointed at his belly, but no one noticed his horse or him. Not even a light flickered. That was good, because he wasn't going back to the Gibbons. Alma had argued with him, saying Katie was right, that he couldn't stay there. Roy had stood there nodding his head in agreement. He'd gone to his room, but the more he thought about the stranger, the more determined he became. Something strong pushed him to his feet. He'd found himself riding Biscuit with a bedroll tied to the back.

He'd sleep on the porch every night until he knew the stranger had moved on.

". . .work in town." Soft words floated through the night air. Katie's voice. Who was she talking to? He sat up and considered walking into the yard to see if there were shadows or light. She hadn't sounded scared but would be if she looked out the window and saw him. No, better stay where he was. It wasn't any of his business.

He'd almost fallen asleep when he heard a sneeze, followed by two more. He perched on his elbows and looked around. He was sure it came from Katie's room but if it hadn't. . .that was enough for him to pull his boots on, grab his shotgun, and take a walk. The moonlight made seeing easy. Nothing seemed out of place. Relieved, he headed back to the front of the house.

Someone stood by the door.

And it wasn't one of the Tuckers.

"Miss Tucker!"

A pounding on the door sent Katie flying from her bed. She met Henry and Oma in the hallway.

"What time is it?" Henry rubbed his eyes.

"Late. Stay here. I'm getting Papa's gun—"

"You there!"

Katie jumped at a voice different from the first. There were two of them. Her heart palpitated against her chest so hard she was sure there would be bruises. What could she do against two men?

Thump. Bump. Crash. The sounds and grunts went on forever, yet she stood rooted to the landing. The men were fighting.

Henry whipped around her and charged down the stairs.

"Stop! Don't go out there!"

"I have to. I'm the man of the house."

Oma held out her wrapper. "Take this and go after him. That boy don't have any sense. Get your papa's gun. Don't be afraid to use it."

Katie nodded, yanking the wrapper around her, and ran after Henry. *God, this isn't right. Why did you take Papa from us?*

She found Henry on the front porch. The fight had ended. No need for the gun. The moonlight lit their rescuer's face. Pete held on to the man who had come earlier.

She chewed her bottom lip, trying to understand what she was seeing. She pulled Henry close. "Mr. Dent, what are you doing?"

"Protecting you."

"You lied. Said your pa didn't need me. That ain't true. He's dead." The man's lip was bleeding. He wavered on his feet and slumped to the floor.

Pete jerked him up. "You aren't staying. You're drunk. Get on your horse and ride out."

"Don't got one. Lost him in a poker game. Just want the job that was promised to me. And I mean to get it."

Chapter 6

Katie shivered. What did he mean by "he'd get the job?" She'd already told him no.

"You won't work here or anywhere in this town, the way you're acting." Pete held on to the man's arm. "Henry, get the wagon. We're taking him in to the sheriff."

"No, please. Not there. I won't come back, at least not like this."

"Not like anything. Miss Tucker said you aren't needed, so there isn't a reason to return."

Katie stiffened. She should be the one giving the orders, or at least Henry. "Mr. Dent, what if you let him sober up and get clean? If he can do that and come back acting civilized, perhaps we can have him help?"

"Doing what?"

"Fixing the barn. Maybe he's fallen on hard times and needs the help of Christians." Had she said that? She had no money for wages.

"How will you pay him?"

"I—I was thinking about that. I won't." Not only wouldn't she pay him, she couldn't, and Pete knew it. Still something nudged her to offer this man a place. Oma always said to listen to the voice in your heart because it was probably God nudging you.

"I ain't workin' for free." The words were slurred, but the message clear.

"Mister, the only pay you'll receive is a place to lay your head, and meals. When Mr. Dent feels you're sober and worth paying, he'll help you find a job." Katie licked her lips. She'd never been so nervous speaking words that made sense. Maybe she needed a second chance to prove herself, too.

"Don't take orders from a woman either." The man spat on the porch.

Pete let go of him. He tumbled, landing on the glob of tobacco he'd just spat. "First thing you'll do is clean up this mess. Then a bath. We'll work on manners while you're here."

"Where do you think he's going to be sleeping, Miss Tucker?" Pete glanced down at the man then back to her. "I don't imagine you want him in the house any more than you wanted me."

"Why, he can sleep on the porch, next to you, as you seem to find that a reasonable place to lay your head at night."

"They can sleep in my room." Henry stood on the bottom step, making him taller than his sister. "That way I can keep an eye on both of them, protecting you and Oma."

Katie's heart fluttered. She wanted Henry to feel like the man of the house, but his suggestion that both of those men—one of them drunk—should sleep down the hall from her. . . .

"Nonsense." Oma had come up behind her. "Henry, if you want to sleep with them, you can sleep out here, too. Mr. Dent, I'd get that man scrubbed clean before morning. He'll need some clean clothes. Don't suppose he's brought any with him?"

"I've no idea. We'll ask him later." Pete scratched his head. "Looks about my size. Guess it would be the Christian thing to loan him something to wear while his get washed."

Katie looked back at the man on the porch. His eyes were closed and he snored. He didn't seem quite so scary. "Oma, it is almost morning."

"Then there's no time to waste. Let's get water on the stove. Henry, you and Pete drag the washtub out close to the pump and start filling it. Once that's done, drag him over. Doesn't matter to me if he goes in with his clothes.

Might as well wash everything at once." She took Katie's arm. "We'll get ready for the day. After breakfast, we'll decide if we need to send him on his way or give him another chance."

"Time to wake up." Pete roused W.D. enough to stand, but not for long from the way he wobbled. Pete draped an arm around his neck to support him and half dragged, half carried him to the waiting tub. He would enjoy watching W.D.'s face when his body hit the water. "Stand back, Henry. He's going to wake up mad."

Standing W.D. at the end of the tub, Pete let go. The man fell backward into the cold water.

"What in the—"

Pete plunged his hands into the water and grabbed W.D. by his shoulders, pulling his face close to his. "Watch your mouth, or you'll be walking back to town in soggy britches."

W.D. relaxed.

Figuring the fight had left him, Pete let go and stepped back. "Humph. You've landed in a soft place for sure. Anyone else would've sent you to jail."

The screen slammed behind Henry. "Katie sent soap. Sorry Mister, it isn't Saturday but she said you had to scrub like it was." He handed him a small sliver instead of a bar. "She said to keep this. If you need more, I'm to get it."

W.D. grimaced and took it. "I didn't want to put anyone out, just wanted a job."

"And you've got one, but first you have to prove your worth." Pete didn't like the idea of this man hanging around Katie, but right now she called the shots. "Soon as you're clean and scrubbed, we'll get started building a lean-to, where we'll both sleep."

"I have clothes in my pack. I had it last night. Did you see it?" W.D. unbuttoned the top of his shirt. "Wouldn't feel too good to walk around in wet clothes. As hot as it is already, by noon, I'll be steaming like a kettle."

"Didn't see one. Henry, you mind running down the lane? Take a look. See if he dropped it."

"Yes, sir. I'll be quick." Henry took off.

Pete glared at W.D. "I'd rather not, but I'll loan you clothes if yours can't be found."

W.D. nodded. "Appreciate that."

"Now that you're sobering up, you and me are going to converse." Pete straightened, rubbed his hand through his hair, missing his hat. Without it, he didn't feel dressed. He stared at W.D. Something about him seemed familiar, but he couldn't place the man.

"You mind if I wash up without you gawking at me?" W.D. had stopped undressing.

"Just want to make sure you're fit for the job and you don't leave until we've had our chat."

"I ain't going anywhere. That's the point of me being

here, remember? I came to get the job I was offered."

"And it's up to me if you stay."

In the kitchen, Katie hovered near the doorway, trying to listen. Her fingernails found their place between her front teeth.

"Katie, stop worrying those fingers. You'll have them bleeding again." Oma tied an apron around her waist. "Let's get breakfast made. The coffee's about ready. When Henry comes in, we'll send him out with some. That will help that man clear his head."

"I'm not sure one cup will be enough. I've never seen anything like that. A man fallen down, so drunk, he goes to sleep with his face in a wad of chewed tobacco." Katie slipped her apron over her head. "Did I do the right thing? What if he is more than a drunk? What if he's dangerous and will murder us while we sleep?"

Oma patted her cheek. "Schatzi, Mr. Dent is here. If he thinks the man needs to leave, he'll tell us. I think God put those earlier words in your mouth."

"Why?"

"Because usually such things make you chew your fingers. Instead, God opened your mouth and you offered Christian charity." She spun Katie around and tied her apron strings.

"I never would've thought of it that way." Her hand

went back to her mouth, but she forced it away. She needed to change. She could no longer allow the things that scared her to keep her from being who God meant her to be. "Oma, would you pray God will make me more courageous, like Rahab?"

"The harlot? It's an odd thing to ask for, but yes, I will ask God, as I have many times, to give you calm nerves." Her wiry eyebrows scrunched together. "Make no mistake, that's the only thing I'm praying for. Rahab turned out to be a blessing, but we don't need to have you imitating her early ways."

"Oma! I'd never!"

"See that you don't. I believe once W.D. gets cleaned up, he and Mr. Dent are going to be fighting to see who wins your hand. And you'll see W.D. is going to be every bit as good looking as Mr. Dent."

Katie felt the warmth rising in her cheeks. "What a thing to say! They won't have any interest in me, you'll see." But what if they did? She wanted Mr. Dent to be the winner. Dare she hope to imagine what it would feel like to be a bride? She twisted a loose curl in her hand. No. She'd buried that desire. No use lighting the fire of hope now. She stuck the wayward tress back into the bun where it belonged.

Chapter 7

She'd wrestled all night, asking God to help her make a choice between searching trees for beehives and being a waitress. No heavenly directions came. She had to choose. The fear of one had to be less than the other. *God, please, there has to be another way.* Again she was met with silence. Looking for work at the diner won. Katie made it to town, her shoes coated in dust, but she hoped that wouldn't keep her from getting hired. With the weight equal to an anvil on each of her shoulders, she pushed through the door.

The smells, smoke, and sudden silence of forks no longer clanking against plates greeted her, turning her stomach. Every eye was directed her way. Her hands shook at her sides. She clasped them together, holding them close to her chin—then realized she must look as if she were getting ready to lead everyone in prayer. Slowly she relaxed her grip and let her hands slide against her skirt, where they had been.

"Miss Tucker? Are you here for breakfast?"

Penny Otto. They had gone to school together. The heaviness on Katie's shoulders slid away as she walked to the counter where her friend stood. "No." Her gaze fell from Penny to the pine plank floor. "I'm looking for work."

"Are you sure? The only need we have is for the breakfast shift. You'd have to take orders and serve food to a rough group of hard-to-work-with men. You'll have to talk to a lot of men that like to flirt with pretty girls."

Katie searched her friend's face and saw concern. Or was it doubt that she could do the job? "Will you be here?"

"Every day but Sunday."

"I'd like to try."

"It doesn't pay much, and the work is harder than you're used to." Penny's face flushed. "I don't mean you can't do it. It's like harvest time every morning, and I know you've done that."

"Harvest is only one time a year."

"Yes, and this comes every day. And on each one, there is someone who will take a likin' to you and make you miserable, and there won't be anything you can do but smile, rebuff them, and refill their coffee cup."

"Why do you do it then?"

"When I told Papa I'm picking my own husband, he said I had to work here, because sitting around the house cost him money." Penny wiped at the counter with a rag. "I'll be leaving as soon as I find the right man. So, do you think you can be here before the sun rises?"

"You don't have to ask your father first?"

"No. But don't think Papa will let you stay if you can't do the work." Penny frowned. "He'll make you leave, in front of everyone, if you don't get the orders right. Papa's a bit," she leaned in and whispered, "difficult to work for sometimes."

Pete had worked on the barn all morning with W.D. and Henry. Katie had left early, looking like she'd drunk a pint of sour milk.

"Henry, where'd Katie go?"

"She's looking for a job at the diner." Henry wiped the sweat from his forehead and then handed some nails to Pete. "You know why, right?" He kept his voice low, as if he didn't want W.D. to hear.

"Because she needs money. She ought to do well waiting tables." Pete pounded a nail into the board that sided the barn.

"Doubt it. She doesn't like to be around people. That's why Papa bought the bees, so she wouldn't have to talk to anyone."

"Bees? He paid for the bees buzzing around the rose bushes?"

"Yes, sir. That and a bunch of stuff that goes with making them stay on our farm. He was going to show me how to take care of them this summer." Henry's eyes filled with tears. "Guess that ain't going to happen."

Pete looked away to allow Henry time to clear his eyes without embarrassment. He put in a few more nails. The barn was coming together, but he still wasn't happy about W.D. being here. So far they'd worked fine together, as long as they worked on opposite sides of the barn, but at some point they were going to meet in the middle.

"I don't get it. What do the bees have to do with Katie? And with her not liking bein' around people?"

"Papa bought them for Katie because she'd told him about how making honey and selling it could bring in good money, and he knew she wouldn't ever get married because, well—you know."

"No, I don't. Explain it to me. What's wrong with her?" Pete's heart cracked a little for Katie's pain. It must hurt her something fierce to know her family thought she wouldn't get married.

"She can't talk to anyone without getting all shaky inside, especially anyone who's come to court her. She gets all red in the face, bursts into tears, and gets a headache." Henry shook his head.

Pete almost laughed. Katie was shy, but that didn't mean

she'd never get married. She hadn't met the man who could get her talking. Though she'd talked to him and W.D. this past week. Could it be she didn't see either of them as being the marrying kind? He'd have to change her mind.

"Katie is a sensitive creature, Papa said, and we had to help her find a way to take care of herself. Guess it's up to me now to figure out how to do that."

"She doesn't like bees." Pete's memory had him back with her in his arms, the day she ran from one.

"No. She's scared of them. She got stung, before any of the bees and equipment came to raise them. Papa never told her about them, afraid she wouldn't leave the house if she knew they were living by the creek."

"Doesn't she ever go there?"

"Nope, I told her that's my special place, and I don't want no girls there." Henry frowned. "Papa said I might want to take a girl there someday. But he was wrong."

"I think your papa knew what he was talking about. It's all about the right time for things to happen."

But Mr. Tucker was wrong about Katie. Pete had an even stronger desire to reach out, protect, and love her, as soon as he broke through her turtle-tough shell.

Pete and Henry stood at the edge of the clearing, near Sugar Creek. Pete counted twelve hives. "Your pa must have thought this bee business would work.

"He said it would make us a lot of money once the honey gets out of those hives." Henry tugged Pete's arm. "I ain't afraid of a bee like Katie, but I figure there's hundreds of them in those boxes."

"Might be. Did you say there is a hat?"

"Papa bought all kinds of stuff."

"It wasn't in the barn, was it?" If it were then getting what they needed would cost. How much, he didn't know.

"I thought it was, but I found it in the woodshed. Katie never goes in there, so I'm guessing that's why Papa put it there. There's a book in Papa's office on how to get the honey out of those hives." Henry frowned. "It probably has big words that I don't know. You know how to read?"

Though taken aback by the question, Pete had a feeling he shouldn't laugh. He'd been taught to read at the orphanage. In fact, he liked reading. "Sure do. Think you can get that book for me?"

"Yes, sir. I'll get it now, while Katie is gone. I don't want her to see it. We don't want to upset her—that's what Papa always said."

Pete couldn't understand why Henry and his father thought Katie was so weak. He'd seen her during the fire, and then again, telling W.D. to go away. She hadn't seemed sensitive then. But Henry was in charge, so he wouldn't insist on telling Katie. Yet.

"Have you figured out what we'll do with the honey?

We can't hide that from her."

"Nope. Guess I'll need to do some thinking on it." Henry grinned. "I know she'll be happy when we show her the bees. She thinks Papa let them go."

Chapter 8

Heavy knives scraped against china plates, and male voices rumbled around Katie. Her hair slid out of its pins. This morning she'd left before sunrise. Oma agreed to handle breakfast while Katie worked, though she had to listen to another lecture about trusting God and not rushing before answers were clear.

So far she had backed away from a man who said she smelled nice and asked her to come closer so he could get a good whiff of her, and another who winked and mentioned the better the service, the bigger his tip. Both encounters made her skin itch. Why hadn't she waited for God's answer? Because she was in charge of taking care of the family, that's why. God had only brought two extra mouths to feed. Shame filled her. She was grateful to Alma for sending Pete. It was the other one she'd like to send away.

"Missy. My coffee's cold." The man she'd nicknamed Mr. Cold Cup pounded the table, making the silverware jump.

It was the third time she'd refilled that man's cup since he'd come in. She gave him a half grin. "I'll be right there." Several plates waited on the ledge behind the counter— her orders were up. Every time she turned, more platters waited. Penny was right. This was harder than harvest. There hadn't been one woman come in this morning.

"Hard time keeping up?" Penny handed her two plates, filled with eggs, potatoes, and bacon.

"The man in the corner seems to need a lot of coffee." The smell of the bacon toyed with the hunger in her stomach. She hadn't had time for breakfast before leaving home.

"He's trying to make you cry. He's done that with everyone we've hired." Penny snatched the coffee urn. "I'll take care of him. Get those platters where they belong, then hang back and watch."

"You bothering my waitress, Robert?" Penny strolled over to his table.

"She's not fast enough. My coffee's cold." He held up his cup.

Penny tipped the pot. "Drink faster and leave the help alone. I can't afford to lose anyone, so be nice like your mother taught you."

Robert smirked. "I'd be plenty nice for you, Penny." He tugged the side of her apron.

Penny grazed the hot pot against his arm.

He yanked away his hand. "Careful, missy."

"That goes both ways. I'm not here for you to be touching. I'm not your wife, and no, before you ask, I have no interest in marrying you."

Katie watched with horror. She'd never be able to act or speak like that to anyone.

"I heard Dent's buying the Tucker place. I guess that's why Katie's working here."

Hearing her name, she stilled. Not wanting to take part in the whispered conversation, she tried to move on, but couldn't. She didn't know the raspy-voiced man and wanted to know why he had said that.

"He's moved in already and rebuilding the barn. I know he's been looking for a place. Guess he found one. Probably for the best. Nobody there to work it anyway." The heavyset man dropped his knife against the plate edge.

Her legs trembled. Pete was trying to steal the farm. Her nervous stomach tumbled. The air thinned.

While she struggled to take a breath, Penny pushed past her. "What's burning?"

Smoke billowed from the kitchen. A fire. Not again. The room spun. She grasped and found nothing to keep her from hitting the floor.

The rumble of wheels came down the lane. It didn't sound like Roy's wagon. The wheels weren't squeaking. Too light for a delivery wagon. Pete stepped away from the barn to look.

Dr. Pickens pulled up with Katie on the bench next to him, her face the color of ash.

Pete ran to the carriage. "What happened? Is she all right?"

"Too much excitement at the diner. There was a fire and Katie passed out. Stew Rutherford caught her before she hit the floor."

With great care, Pete lifted Katie from the carriage and held her in his arms.

"You smell nice." She rested her head on his shoulder.

"I don't think so, but thank you anyways."

"Take her inside and put her to bed. I gave her a dose of laudanum to calm her down," Dr. Pickens said. "She was crying and shrieking. I don't think she ought to be working there. It's too much for her. I admire her for trying, but there's always a chance of a fire in the kitchen. Her father wouldn't approve."

"Maybe not, but she's trying hard to make the farm work. I'm proud of her, given she has trouble talking to people. Yet she hasn't once complained." He shifted her in his arms, causing her eyes to open wide. "Shh. It's okay. I'm taking you inside, and your grandmother will take care of you."

She reached up and stroked his cheek.

Dr. Pickens coughed. "Best get her inside to her grandmother before she does something you'll both regret."

"Thank you for bringing her home. You'd be welcome, if you care to stay."

"I'm on my way to Alma's, but maybe next time."

Pete propped pillows around Katie's head and stepped back from the couch. "Time for you to take a nap. I bet you'll have some sweet dreams."

"I'm dreaming of what it would be like to have you kiss me." Her head fell back. Her eyes closed. A tiny snore escaped from her nose, making him smile. Someday he was going to kiss the tip of that perfect nose.

"Oma, what am I to do? I don't want to sell the farm." Katie held her head between her hands. The stabbing pain didn't want to let up.

"Drink tea. The more you do, the better you'll feel. About this other matter, I do not know." Oma patted Katie's arm. "God does and He has a plan. You'll see."

A knock on the door sent lightening through her head. "Come in, but quietly, please."

"I'm sorry. I wanted to see how you were feeling this morning." Pete held his hat in his hand.

He was so tall, and she remembered thinking how comforting it was to lay her head on his shoulder. She felt her face flush. Was he thinking about that, too? "I'll be fine. Though I don't know what I'll do to pay you." She stood, her chair screeching against the pine floor. "Are you planning on buying this farm? I heard that yesterday, and I want to know now if you're here to help or hurt us."

Pete looked at the floor then back at her, with the softest brown eyes she'd ever seen. "No. I'm looking for a place of my own, that's true, but this is Henry's farm."

"So you're leaving as soon as we get the barn built and the crops harvested?"

Henry popped through the door. "You can't leave. You promised to help me with the—"

"And I will, Henry. I can't stay here. You're the—"

"Help him with what?" Katie crossed the kitchen floor and poked Pete in the chest. "What are you teaching him that you don't want me to know about?"

"Uhm, nothing. Girls, maybe." Pete's face turned red. He tugged on his ear. "I promised I'd show him how to ask a girl out. Henry, are you watching?"

"Yes, sir."

"Miss Tucker, would you please go with me to the Fourth of July fireworks?"

"That's it? You just say her name? What if she says no?"

"Ah, but Henry, what if she says—"

"Yes, Mr. Dent. I'd enjoy being escorted to the big doings at the park."

Pete winked at Henry. "That's how it's done. Now let's

get back to putting the barn together."

Katie had a feeling she'd been left out of something else. But she didn't care. Her headache had flown away. She had a fellow. A mighty fine one at that.

Chapter 9

Sweaty and hot, Katie pushed her sleeves to her elbows and walked through a grove of trees, trying to follow a bee. At a distance. She'd seen one fly this way and knew from reading they often built hives in trunk hollows. If she could locate at least one hive, maybe with Henry's help they could harvest and sell the honey. It was going for a good price, and like she'd told Papa, it was a good investment.

Still, they were bees and they stung. She slowed her search. If she wasn't willing to be stung, why did she want her brother to be? She sniffled. Something about this time of year made her head hurt and nose twitch. She sneezed. Fearing a headache, she turned back to the house. She'd search another day.

This afternoon she'd rather be deciding what to wear to the Fourth of July celebration than looking for bees.

She wanted to wear the blue taffeta dress. Papa bought it for her when he'd traveled to St. Louis to visit Doc Pickens in April, when he was there studying. She'd yet to wear it, not finding an occasion worthy of the way it made her feel. Beautiful, tall, and almost courageous.

Silly. Courage comes from God, not a dress. But maybe He used it to show her? Sometimes when she tried to figure out what God was all about, she came away more confused than when she started. But Papa always said, *Go back to the beginning and what you know.*

She knew God loved her, that He sent His Son to die for her sins, and He wanted His children to be happy. Well the dress made her happy, so it must have come from God. Pete made her happy, too—she wanted to stretch her arms wide and turn like a five year old until she could no longer stand up. But she was much too old for that behavior and, besides, her head was beginning to hurt.

Bassler Park dressed with kerosene lamps made the night feel like a fairy tale, and she a princess. The wavy light highlighted the golden tones in Pete's brown eyes. Would he be her first kiss? Katie didn't know what to do with the feelings piling up inside, like logs in a dam. Pete held on to her elbow as if it were treasure. The night air was soft, not too sticky. The fireworks popped, cracked, and sizzled; lighting up the sky with their sparks. At first the smoky smell and bright light twisted her stomach enough to make her feel faint. Then the beauty of it struck Katie. Papa would want her to enjoy this, and to enjoy Pete. He'd be happy she'd caught someone's eye. Probably relieved that she might not end up alone after all.

Soon the sky exploded with the bright zigzagging streams of fireworks and then grew dark.

"Did you like it?" Pete squeezed her hand. "The smoke didn't bother you, did it? I should have considered that it might."

"I enjoyed it, very much." His consideration of her feelings increased her desire to love him.

"Katie, we need to find Henry and get back."

And then she turned back into the farm girl who lived in Trenton. "Isn't he supposed to meet us at the buggy when the fireworks ended?"

"He might not think it's over until he and his friends inspect for those that didn't go off."

"Henry's not like that. You'll see. He'll be there." He'd better be there. She'd hate for Pete to think Henry would be disrespectful.

They strolled up the sparsely lit path, passing the brewery. From the shadows, a man stepped in front of them.

Katie gasped then settled when she recognized W.D.

"Miss Tucker, when am I gettin' paid?" W.D. stood, arms crossed, blocking the path.

Katie sought Pete's arm.

"You know the deal, W.D. You get money later. Right now you get a place to sleep and food to eat."

"Says you, Dent. I bet you're getting paid in other ways. How's those lips of hers? Soft as a—"

Pete lunged forward. "Don't talk about her like that. Have you been drinking?"

"What if I am?"

"I'm not fighting a drunk." He stepped away. "Find somewhere else to sleep tonight. Tomorrow come and get your things. You're done at the Tucker place."

"I'm sorry, Katie. I shouldn't have fought with him at all." Pete helped her into the carriage.

Henry came panting up to them. "I heard there was a fight and Pete walloped W.D. Why'd you do that? Sure wish I hadn't of missed that. That's more exciting than looking for dead fireworks."

"You were supposed to come here after they ended." Katie glanced at Pete. "It seems tonight no one is who I thought they were." She pulled the hem of her dress close to her feet. "Get in, Henry, and be careful not to step—"

"On your most beautiful dress ever—that you've been

saving for the perfect time. I know." Henry climbed in.

Pete let that information sink in. She'd worn her best for him. Something loosened in his heart. Was God really listening to his prayers?

Chapter 10

After Pete had seen Katie and Henry home, and taken care of the horse and buggy, he couldn't help but stare at the empty bunk where W.D. should be. Anger surged through him as he remembered the hateful words the man had shouted at Katie. He had better not show up here tonight, or Pete would finish what was started.

He yanked off his boots and tossed them on the floor at the foot of his bed. God had judged people when they were wrong, so why feel bad about his own indignation? Feeling righteous, he picked up his Bible and scooted close to the lamp.

Reading Judges would prove him right. He opened the book, intending to head straight there. Instead his hand stilled at Ephesians, Chapter four. He wanted to keep turning but feeling a push to read, he did so. "Be ye angry, and sin not: let not the sun go down upon your wrath." The sun wasn't even out when he ran into W.D. Did it mean he could go to sleep without worry?

He read further: "Let all bitterness, and wrath, and anger, and clamour and evil speaking, be put away from you, with all malice: And be ye kind one to another, tenderhearted, forgiving one another, even as God for Christ's sake hath forgiven you."

No way he was going to sleep easy with those holy words running through his brain. He set the Bible on his bunk. Unease poked his shoulder. A walk, and a talk, with God was in order. He put on his shoes and grabbed the lamp. He might as well check on the bees while he was conversing.

Katie sat on Oma's bed, tracking the tiny stitching of the Dresden Plate quilt with her finger while her grandmother brushed her hair. Something she hadn't done in a long time. Tonight she longed for a mother, but grandmother was the closest she'd ever have. Did she experience the same kind of fluttery feelings when grandfather courted her? She wanted to ask but didn't know if that would make Oma sad.

The brush pulled against Katie's tangled, wavy locks. Maybe she shouldn't have pinned it so well, but it was the only way she could get it under her hat.

"The singing was nice enough at the picnic, but nothing like the time they put on the opera."

"The *Pinafore*? I can only imagine what that must have been like. I wish I could've seen it, Oma." The performance had been given by locals talented enough that the older people still talked about it with great enthusiasm every time a concert was held at the park.

"The Trenton Brass Band was as good." Oma stopped brushing. "What's the matter, Schatzi? You not have a good time tonight?"

Katie whipped around and faced her grandmother. "It was—I can't find the words! The lights in the park were like jewels, and being with Pete made me. . . ."

"Lit a fire in you, did he?" Sparkles danced in Oma's eyes. "I knew he was a good man. Patient with you, not worried about your nervousness. I've been praying for God to send a man like him for you. I knew your father wasn't right."

"What are you saying?"

"He loved you, remember that. But he didn't think you'd ever find a husband, with your condition. That's why he wanted to make sure the bees were a success. If you could make the honey business work, he knew you'd be able to do anything you set your mind on. It was hard on him when you were so afraid. He was praying for God to send a man who could see past the skittishness."

"And you think that's Pete?"

"Would he make you happy?"

Katie wanted to say no, but the way her lips were stretching past the normal corners of her mouth would give her away.

"Good. Then we will pray Mr. Dent asks you to be his wife." Oma wasted no time. Her head bent, hands folded, she began her plea to her Lord.

Should he have brought the smoker with him? Pete considered going back, but he didn't plan on getting close to the hives. It was a destination, more than anything. He'd not go close. Besides, he had a nudge or a shove between his shoulder blades urging him to turn back and head to town. It had to be from God because the last thing he wanted to do was talk with W.D., especially if he had continued drinking.

Sticks broke underfoot. Something skittered off the path in front of him. He hadn't brought his gun. Foolish mistake to come out after dark with it. Coyotes and other night critters—what was that?

He stood stone still. Buzzing. Loud buzzing. Buzzing that shouldn't be coming his way this time of night. From the sound there had to be more than one bee headed right at him.

He turned to run.

The bees followed.

He held the light to his face, hoping the flame would scare them. It heightened their anger. As he ran he twisted the knob, extinguishing the light. But he couldn't put out the fire on his skin.

He dropped the lantern and ran for the creek while slapping at his shirt trying to kill the bees that found a way into it. He bit back a yell as another one found his skin. It came out as a whimper. Wading into the water, the mud sucked at his feet and determined bees came at his head. He flopped forward, submerging his head, over and over, until the last bee had either died or returned to the hive.

Soaking, and shaking from the experience, he now understood Katie's very real fear. He also got God's message. Once he changed clothes, he'd be headed to town to find W.D.

Chapter 11

Pete turned Biscuit down Railroad Street and headed toward White's Saloon, figuring it to be the most likely place to find W.D. Every movement on the horse made his chest ache. He wanted to be back on his cot, soaking the painful areas with baking soda, but he wasn't about to argue with God. At least, he wasn't taking a chance that God wasn't the one sending him on the hunt for W. D.

He liked riding through town at night. Sometimes a curtain hadn't been closed and the light inside gave him a peek of what he wanted his life to look like. A father hugging a little child, or a head bowed in prayer. He had quite a bit saved and wanted to ask Katie to marry him; but what would they do about the farm? It was Henry's of course, but he was too young to leave alone with it.

The noise coming from inside White's Saloon meant the celebration continued. He slowed Biscuit and whispered a prayer that he wouldn't find W. D. inside and, if he did, the man would be reasonable about coming outside for a conversation. What that would be about, he wasn't sure. He'd depend on God for those words. He tied Biscuit to the hitching post and went inside.

The kerosene lights turned the smoke-filled room into a thick yellow cloud. Glass mugs clinked against the bar top, laughter thundered from the corner. Pete walked past tables until he found W. D. alone, hat resting next to an empty mug and spilled beer.

Pete slid the heavy wooden chair out and sat in front of W.D. "I came to talk."

"Not interested." He didn't look up.

If only it were easy and he could say, "Me either." But his heart felt heavy, and he couldn't up and leave. "Truce? Let's go outside and watch for the train, maybe talk instead of using fists?"

W.D. cocked his head. "Watch for the train? That brings back an old memory. Why not?" He picked up his hat and shoved it on.

The two of them stepped outside and found a quieter spot on the porch. Both of them leaned over and anchored their hands to the banister. Pete knew he held on, unsure of what he'd say. W.D. probably held on to steady himself or keep from swinging at him.

"Why'd you come looking for me? You don't seem like someone to search out a fight."

"I'm not. Just something I felt I needed to do. Let's start over, you and me. Why don't you tell me what W.D. stands for?" Somewhat relieved at coming up with an easy question, he let go of the banister.

"William Dentice. Dentice was my last name before I was adopted."

Pete no longer noticed the bee stings. He couldn't feel anything. He'd been searching for his brother for years, and now he was standing next to him.

In bed, Katie rolled one way, then the other. Her nightdress crawled past her hip and cinched her waist. She tugged it back in place.

The loan date circled in red was fast approaching, and the only money coming in came from the chickens. If they had another cow they could sell the milk. But they didn't.

Maybe she could nail up a notice, offering to take in ironing. But then she'd be taking money away from the widow with seven kids.

If she could find a hive, there had to be honey. She could sell it and the wax quick enough to make a payment to the bank. But she had to face her fears. Did she know enough about beekeeping? She knew a lot from reading the book, like the bee that came after her on the porch the day Pete saved her was a worker bee. She sat up and scratched at a mosquito bite. The crickets sang outside her window. Had Papa bought the smoker and netted hat, too? Maybe even enough hives to build an apiary?

What if all of those things that could save the farm were in the barn when it burned? She fell back on the bed. Her eyes stung. *It's too much, God. I can't do this alone.* She hoped for a calming verse to pop into her mind but it didn't. If her mind would settle, she could sleep, but how could that happen, when all she could hear was Papa died thinking she'd failed?

She tossed the blankets aside and lay on her stomach, letting her pillow contain the weight of her worry tears. In the light of day, she knew Papa was in heaven and probably knew how her story was going to turn out. But she was still here, and life was, well, unsettling.

She fell asleep and dreamed of watching the farm being auctioned. Pete couldn't be found and W.D. bought her memories.

"Billy?" Pete pushed the name through his lips, still not believing this drunken man could be his brother.

"Nobody calls me that." W.D. growled and let go of the banister, his hand balled into a fist. "That's a child's name. I stopped being one of those a long time ago."

Pete dropped his gaze and studied his broken thumbnail. He had to tell him. He took a deep breath. "I think you might be my younger brother."

"Naw, your name's Dent. I had a big brother, but I can't remember his first name. I've been searching for another Dentice but came up empty."

"I changed it." Pete's voice cracked. "I looked for you. I went to the farm where you were supposed to be."

"Wasn't there. That family moved to Kansas and used me for labor. Took out on my own when I was fifteen. Came back this way about a year ago."

About the time Pete quit searching.

"Why'd you change your name?"

"No one could say it."

"That's some truth. I'm sorry about saying what I did about Miss Tucker. You care for her, easy enough to see that. Don't know why that bothered me so much."

"Maybe you're looking for a home as much as me?" How would he explain all of this to Katie? Would she want to be associated with him once she knew W.D. was his brother? If she didn't accept him, could he walk away from her? He knew he wasn't going to let W.D. slip out of his life again. The pain of losing him twice might erase his desire for living.

"Guess this is where we say good-bye again." W.D.'s voice thickened. "Sure wish I'd have shown up at the Tucker's better behaved."

"No. We're not being separated again. You're coming back with me, and we'll figure out how this is going to work in the morning."

"I don't want to come between the two of you."

"Things will work out. Let's get you on your horse and get back to the farm."

"I want you to know I haven't always been this way." He trailed behind Pete. "The last few years aren't something I'm proud of. I've done things that—"

"Everyone has, Billy." The old name rolled off his tongue with ease. He stopped and turned back. Under all that facial hair was a face he might've recognized. "Make no mistake, there's no one alive that hasn't sinned. That's why we're thankful for God's grace."

"Don't think He has grace enough for me, but I'm sure glad I found you."

"We'll talk about it tomorrow when you can think clearer. Let's go home, brother." He turned his head to hide his tears of thankfulness. God had answered his prayer. Not the way he'd hoped, but it was an answer.

Chapter 12

Pete found Katie fighting a breeze while hanging sheets on the line. "Let me help you with that." He took one corner, stretched it, and waited for her to pin it.

"What's got you helping me with laundry?" She cocked her head. "Not that I don't appreciate it. Hanging sheets is hard enough without the wind whipping them around."

A gust blew the sheet, sticking it to both of them. Laughing, they untangled themselves.

"See what I mean?" Katie fiddled with her hair, fixing a loose pin.

He found her beyond adorable. Sliding a finger under a flyaway strand, he tucked it into place. Then without thought, his lips found hers. The connection could've been lightning forging them forever in that moment. He pulled away and felt a canyon-deep emptiness. "Katie. I'm sorry—"

She reached for him, and settled his lips against hers. Just as quick she broke away. "I'm not. But now I think I shouldn't have done that."

Pete swallowed, took a breath, and willed the fire between them to simmer. "Let's finish this chore. We need to talk."

Katie grabbed another sheet. She didn't look at him. "I know what you are going to say. You aren't interested in having a skittish wife. That's why I kissed you back. I'll never get another one."

He groaned. "You're wrong. I've been wanting to kiss you for a year. But after you hear what I have to say, you may want to send me away." He took the sheet from her hand and put it in the basket. He held her hands in his. "Last night I went looking for W.D. I found him at the saloon."

"I hope you left that dreadful man there."

He let go of her hands. She'd reject him as soon as she knew. He hated choosing, but he couldn't let his brother leave without trying to help him.

"Katie, I know how you feel about W.D., but he's my brother. I thought I'd lost him forever. I can't let that happen again. I'll leave, and Roy will help you find someone to work the farm." He leaned over and kissed the top of her head, hoping she'd say something. When she didn't, he backed away. "I hoped you would be able to forgive him."

He wanted so much to stay. If only she'd say something. Anything that would let him hope there was a chance for them that would include W.D. With great sorrow, he turned and walked away.

He'd kissed her. Topsy-turvyed her world and then tore it apart with his words. Leaving. That's what she heard. The only man who'd ever shown interest in her, that she'd been brave enough to kiss back, hadn't even given her a chance to tell him he could stay.

She didn't know he had a brother.

Henry came running through the sheets. "Katie, have you seen Pete?"

"Stop that! You'll get them dirty! He's in the barn. Pete's leaving. It's the two of us against the bank, Henry." She reached for a clothes pin and tipped the bucket, spilling them on the ground. *Pete had kissed her. Her first kiss, and now he was running away.* If Henry weren't standing there, she'd kick the bucket across the yard.

"Why's he going?" Henry's lip trembled.

Crushed at Henry's pain, Katie pulled him close. "We have each other, Oma, and God. We're going to be okay." But would they? Katie wanted to kneel on the grass and yell at God.

"Henry, Katie." Pete stood behind them.

Katie's heart fluttered. Maybe it wasn't too late. She

held on to Henry but turned to Pete. "We don't want you to leave."

"I came back because I thought about our. . ." He blushed and brushed his fingers over his lips.

Surely he wouldn't say anything about the kiss in front of Henry! Katie jumped in. "If W.D. can change, then we'd like him to stay. Wouldn't we, Henry? Pete, he's your family and you have to try."

"Yeah, besides our project needs finishing." Henry strode in front of Pete. "I can't do it by myself." He straightened his body and wore a serious look. "Besides, I saw you kiss my sister, and I think we've some talking to do. Man to man."

"You're right, Mr. Tucker. If I could speak with you privately, we could discuss the situation while working on the project."

"What are you two up to? And why speak with Henry? You aren't Papa."

Henry's shoulders drooped. "No, but I'm doing the best I can. Come on, Pete. Follow me."

Pete stopped on his way to the house, struck by Katie's beauty. Her blond hair glimmered in the evening sun, where she sat on the back steps, snapping green beans. Soon he'd ask her to be his wife, but first he had to show her the bees. "Come with me. There's something Henry and I have been working on. He wants me to show you."

"What is it?" She snapped the ends off a bean and tossed them into a pan at her feet.

"Always curious, aren't you?" And beautiful. He'd asked Henry if he could marry his sister. Henry said yes, with great enthusiasm. They'd discussed what that meant for the farm, and the two of them came to an agreement. He and Katie would live in the house until Henry married, then build another house.

"Papa said I was worrisome and nervous." She set the beans aside and stood, brushed off her apron, removed it, and draped it over the porch banister.

"I think you are a wise woman, not ready to jump in until you know the facts. That's why Henry and I haven't told you about any of this." He held his hand out and, when she took it once again, felt God answering another prayer.

"You haven't said a word about the big secret."

"Will you trust me enough to follow me to Sugar Creek?" All afternoon he'd been thinking of a romantic way to ask her to marry him. He should have proposed during the fireworks. Henry suggested he buy her doughnuts, but Pete thought that was what Henry would want. He'd ask W.D. if he had any ideas when he turned in tonight.

"That's Henry's place. Don't you know girls aren't allowed?"

"He said it was okay."

"Is it safe?"

"Please, Katie. You need to see this." Pete held out his hand. "I'd like to show you before it gets dark."

"Should I get a lantern?"

"No!" His chest hurt thinking about the night he'd taken one with him.

"Then we'd better hurry so we can get back before the June bugs come out."

They walked in silence to the field by the creek.

Pete stopped just out of sight of the hives. "Remember, you're safe with me. Don't run. Are you ready?"

She nodded but her eyebrows let him know she was worried, along with her strong grip on his hand.

As they grew closer, she gasped. "There's an apiary! Did Papa do this?"

"Yes, and Henry and I have been taking care of them. We have jars of honey stacked in the woodshed."

"Wax, too?" She beamed. "You saved us and the farm. How did you know what to do?" Her eyes widened. "Did you get stung a lot? How much honey did you harvest? Are those all the queen bees Papa bought?"

"God saved you. I read a book." And fought off a swarm of bees. "Yes, I got stung. I forgot how much honey, you can count the jars and yes, those are the Italian queens your father purchased." He smiled down at her. "Anything else?"

"I want to go closer." She stepped forward then turned. "Not by myself!"

No one would call her nervous and skittish now. "I'll be right by your side."

He felt her hand tremble in his. "We can go now. Henry wants you to know that he and I will take care of the bees. All we ask of you is to get the honey into jars."

"I can make hand creams, too." Her nose wrinkled.

Pete had a bad feeling, but before he could do anything, Katie sneezed. Loud. Bees came flying out of their hives, wings sounding like a train. "Run! We've got to get in the creek!"

Katie screamed once, twice, and then they were in the water.

"Put your head under!"

A few minutes later, the bees left, no longer considering them a threat. Katie's hair had come undone and was plastered to her face. Already there were welts forming on her cheeks.

"I'm so sorry! I didn't know they'd come after us if you sneezed."

"Guess we do now. I must look awful with all these stings."

"I love you, Katie Tucker. Honey, will you be my bride?" He plucked the hair from her cheek. "I could call you my honey bride because the bees brought us together."

"Yes! Yes! I'll marry you, Pete Dent."

August came in hot and humid, but Katie didn't care. She and Oma had spent days fixing honey cakes for the wedding today. She wore her mother's wedding gown. It was a perfect fit. Oma said that was a sign she'd found the right man to marry. And that man was waiting for her at the altar.

Henry threaded his arm through hers. "Ready, Katie? Cause I sure am."

Katie swallowed; she couldn't speak. She nodded at her brother and took her first step down the aisle, where Pete waited. Soon she'd be Mrs. Pete Dent.

Christian author Diana Lesire Brandmeyer writes historical and contemporary romances. Author of *Mind of Her Own*, *A Bride's Dilemma in Friendship, Tennessee*, and *We're Not Blended—We're Pureed, A Survivor's Guide to Blended Families*. Once widowed and now remarried, she writes with humor and experience on the difficulty of joining two families, be they fictional or real life. Visit Diana's website: www.dianabrandmeyer.com

The Lumberjack's Bride

Pam Hillman

Chapter 1

The piney woods along Sipsey Creek,
Mississippi, June 1889

Lucy Denson wove her way among the towering pines, her attention focused on the steady buzz of a crosscut saw up ahead.

She hefted the basket, filled with lunch for the lumberjacks, and huffed out a breath, blowing a wispy strand of hair off her face. Why Papa had insisted on returning to Mississippi was beyond her. Of course when her cousin Jack's logging business had taken off and he'd asked for help, Papa had felt obliged to leave Chicago and use his bookkeeping skills to manage the books for Jack and his partner. She wrinkled her brow as the tip of her boot scattered the remains of a rotten log and black beetles scampered out. Seemed like Jack could have found someone else to keep the books.

His own sister, Annabelle, had been a school teacher. She was perfectly capable of tallying a column of numbers. But no, tradition dictated the books had to be managed by a man, so her father had packed up the entire family and moved them all back to Mississippi, and no amount of begging could induce him to let her stay in Chicago.

Tears smarted her eyes.

And just when Deotis Reichart had started to take notice of her. Her father's impetuous midlife crisis had ruined the chance for the life she dreamed of. She pushed thoughts of what she'd left behind in Chicago to the back of her mind, hiked her skirt, and navigated a steep incline. Right now she'd promised her cousin Annabelle she'd deliver thick slabs of roast beef sandwiches and roasted potatoes to the men working on the ridge up ahead. She might not be able to cook, but she was willing to help out in any way she could. She paused and cocked her head, listening for the saws.

And that's when she spotted the spider web stretched between two trees. She stopped and stared, the intricate design eye-catching in its simplicity. She stood transfixed, trying to memorize the pattern so she could repeat it with her crochet needles. She regretted not having anything to sketch the web. After all, she hadn't expected to run into such beauty when she'd ventured into the woods.

The web quivered, and her gaze snapped upward where she spotted a large yellow-and-black spider. She shuddered and stepped back. The web design was fascinating, but she could do without the spider. The spell broken, she veered around the web, left the spider to its business, and started off again. The sooner she delivered the men's lunch, the sooner she could head back to the cook shack, where the smoke from the stove kept the spiders, mosquitoes, and bugs at bay.

And maybe there she could scrounge up a scrap of paper to sketch the web.

"Keep sawing." Eli Everett's muscles ached with fatigue as he pushed the crosscut saw toward his little brother, Josiah.

An amused grunt rumbled through his chest. He'd have to amend his thinking. Josiah had shot up like a green sapling in the last year, and no one would dare call him little anymore. Hard work behind a crosscut saw had honed his muscles until Eli wouldn't want to be caught on his bad side. Not that that was likely to happen. Josiah was as easygoing as a lazy dog in the shade.

A creaking noise interrupted his musing, and his attention focused sharply on the job at hand. He could feel Josiah letting up on his end of the saw, a sure sign his brother thought it was time to make a run for it. Eli gripped the handles and thrust the saw back toward his brother, an unspoken order that they needed to stay with the tree a few minutes longer.

Suddenly the creak turned into a full-fledged groan that didn't let up. They paused, easing the saw out to protect it from damage. His head tilted back. He lifted his gaze upward, skimming the tall, long length of the loblolly pine. The top swayed, and he nodded at Josiah.

"Timber!" Josiah took off at a run.

Eli turned, and that's when he saw her.

Right in the path of the severed pine tree.

Head down, she picked her way toward him, a wide-brimmed straw hat shading her features, pink gauzy ribbons tied under her chin swaying gently in the breeze. Her gaze lifted and met his. In a split second, Eli took in everything about her, from the brilliant blue of her eyes, hair as pale as fresh-cut lumber, the light-colored sprigged skirt cinched about her narrow waist, to the white shirtwaist and crocheted shawl draped across her shoulders, even the basket looped over her arm.

Then he was moving, running toward her.

The large, brawny man charged at Lucy like a raging bull. She froze.

Before she could think or move, her gaze shifted up and over his head to the tree, big enough to flatten half-a-dozen cable cars on the streets of Chicago. The tree swayed then, almost in slow motion, began to fall—directly toward her. A scream bubbled up from her chest, only to cut off abruptly as the lumberjack slammed into her. The impact knocked the breath from her, but she felt them rolling, everything a hazy blur as her straw hat was ripped away, and twigs jerked pins from her hair.

Her crazy, tilting world stopped, and she found herself on the forest floor, the lumberjack's broad frame hunched over her, sheltering her. She reached to push him away, but froze, when over his shoulder, she caught a glimpse of the monster tree hurtling toward earth. She whimpered, squeezed her eyes shut, and tucked her face against the roughness of the man's work shirt.

Please, God, don't let me die.

A mighty shudder shook the ground.

Lucy didn't move; she barely even let herself breathe. Everything slammed into her stunned brain at once. The fact that she was alive. The utter stillness of the man who'd protected her with his life. The quiet of the forest. No sound. Nothing. Not a leaf stirred, no birds chirped, not even a cricket could be heard.

Then she felt it, or heard it. She wasn't sure.

The rapid staccato beat of the lumberjack's heart where her ear pressed against his broad chest. She listened as the rhythm slowed, keeping time with her own heartbeat's gradual return to normal. She pulled in a shuddering breath as the truth of what had almost happened struck her full force. Her rescuer stirred, pushed himself up, and gazed down at her. Shadow-filled dark eyes probed hers, then swept her face.

"Ma'am?" His voice rolled over her, breathless and jagged like the teeth of the crosscut saw he'd tossed aside as he rushed to her rescue. "Are you all right?"

"I—" Lucy stammered, trying to control the trembling that set in. "I—I think so."

Chapter 2

When tears pooled in her liquid blue eyes, Eli panicked. He pushed himself up from the ground, reached for the woman—not much more than a slip of a girl—and stood her on her feet. She swayed, trembling.

"What in heaven's name were you thinking?" He growled, hands anchored on his hips to keep from reaching out to steady her again. If he did, he was afraid she'd dissolve into a puddle of tears at his feet, and then he'd be in a logjam for sure.

"Annabelle sent me—"

"You could have been killed." The more he thought about how close she'd come to getting flattened by that tree, the madder he got. He grabbed her dainty little straw hat off the ground and shoved it at her. "Don't ever do that again."

Her blue eyes flashed fire, and bright pink rushed back into her face which had been pale only moments before. She plopped the hat on her head and shoved her mass of golden curls up under it before crossing her arms and glaring down her pert little nose at him. Or at least it felt like she glared down at him, which was ridiculous since she was a good eight inches shorter than he was. "Rest assured, Mr. Everett, I won't do it again. I'll just leave your lunch on the ground and you can fight the ants for it."

She whirled, lifted her skirts, and marched away.

"Eli?" He glanced over his shoulder. Josiah stood near, looking worried, the basket dangling from one hand. "Is she all right?"

"Yeah. She's fine." Eli jerked his slouch hat off, slapped it against his leg, and huffed out a breath. "Maybe that little scare will teach her to be more careful in the woods."

"Must be Jack's cousin from Chicago." Josiah let out a shrill whistle to call their brothers in for lunch then plopped down on a stump. He dug into the basket, unearthing a thick, juicy-looking roast beef sandwich. "Wasn't Jack's uncle supposed to arrive this week and take over as ink slinger?"

"That's what they said." Eli stared after the young woman as she picked her way through the woods, her pink flower-sprigged dress held clear of the forest floor. Nobody had told him Mr. Denson's daughter was so pretty or that she'd be helping out at the camp kitchen.

Josiah swallowed a bite of his sandwich and nodded in the direction Miss Denson had gone. "You gonna eat your lunch or go tell her she's headed in the wrong direction?"

Eli scowled, slapped his hat on his head, and stomped off after her. The sooner he got her out of the woods and back with Annabelle and Maggie, the sooner he could get his mind back on his work.

As he drew near, she turned, her brow wrinkled in confusion. "I seem to be. . ."

"Lost?" he growled.

"Not exactly lost. Just turned around a bit." A pale pink blush swept over her cheeks, like the gentle sweep of a summer breeze. "If you could just point me in the right direction."

"I'll do better than that. The skid road's this way." Eli gestured toward the road and let her precede him. She hadn't gone three steps before she stumbled over an exposed root. Grabbing her elbow, he kept her upright.

She threw him a grateful glance. "Thank you, Mr. Everett."

"Name's Eli. We don't stand on ceremony around here." Eli didn't bother to ask how she knew who he was. He figured Annabelle had filled her in on every man who worked for Sipsey Creek Lumber and Logging. "You're Miss Denson, aren't you?"

She nodded. "I didn't realize you and your brother were so far away when I volunteered to deliver your lunch. It sounded as if you were right over the ridge from the road."

"Sound carries out here in the woods."

"I realize that now."

Finally, they arrived at the log road, a long swath weaving its way through the pine forest toward base camp. Miss Denson glanced right then left, her brow puckered in a frown. "Which way—"

Eli motioned left and started that way.

Lucy hurried to keep up with Eli Everett's long-legged stride. "I'm sorry for taking you away from your work."

"It's all right." He shrugged.

She *was* sorry, but glad he'd taken it upon himself to show her the way back. She'd been so focused on following the sound of the saw she hadn't really paid attention to her surroundings, and one tree looked much the same as another.

The sound of jingling harnesses reached them, and just around the next bend, she spotted Maggie and Annabelle headed toward them in the wagon they'd driven out to the woods to feed the men. Maggie waved and pulled the wagon to a halt, a look of relief on her face. "Oh, there you are, Lucy. We were getting worried."

Annabelle's gaze swept her from head to toe then

shifted to Eli, one eyebrow lifted in question. Lucy glanced at her dirt-smudged dress, *tsk*ing at a rip in the hem. If her clothes were any indication, she must look a sight. She lifted one hand and made sure her hair was still restrained under her hat. Unless she missed her guess, she'd lost some of her pins, but she couldn't very well repin her hair in front of Mr. Everett.

"I had a bit of an accident. I arrived just as the Everetts—Eli and his brother—finished cutting down a tree."

Annabelle and Maggie gasped in unison. "Are you hurt?"

"I'm fine. Really."

"She almost got killed," Eli growled.

Lucy sighed. "But I didn't. You made sure of that."

"Thank goodness you weren't hurt." Maggie shook her head, looking at Lucy like she should've had more sense than to walk up on two men felling a tree. Well, she'd learned her lesson. She wouldn't do it again. Ever. She eyed her ruined dress, confident she'd avoid the woods completely in the future.

Maggie scooted over on the wagon seat. "Well, we'd better get back to the kitchen. Supper will be here before you know it. And Annabelle isn't feeling well."

For the first time, Lucy noticed how pale her cousin looked. "Annabelle?"

Her cousin smiled wanly and pressed a hand to her midriff. "I'm fine. Just a little nauseated."

Eli handed Lucy into the wagon and tipped his hat. A faint grin played with the edges of his mouth. "Miss Denson, my ma used to ring a cowbell when she brought meals to the woods. We'd all come running like a herd of cattle when we heard Ma's bell. Worked like a charm every time."

"Thank you, Mr. Everett." Lucy inclined her head and smoothed her skirt. "A herd of cattle. I'll keep that in mind."

Long strides took Eli back to where Josiah, Caleb, and Gideon were just finishing up their lunch. Josiah waved him over and handed him a sandwich. "Here. I saved you some. Did you get little Miss Priss back to safety?"

Eli chuckled at Josiah's description of the prim and proper Miss Denson. At least she'd been prim and proper before a tree had almost pinned her to the ground. But even the ripped and torn dress, her smudged face, and disheveled hair hadn't robbed her of her cultured look. "Don't be too hard on her. She's from the city. She couldn't have known how dangerous it could be out here."

"Is she pretty?" Caleb wiped his mouth on his sleeve and grinned.

Gideon snorted. "Even if she was, she wouldn't look twice at you, you big lug."

"Better me than you, that's for sure."

Eli ignored their banter and dug around in the basket

Lucy—Miss Denson—had left with them. He frowned when he unearthed a pinecone. Must have fallen in the basket when the tree toppled from the sky. He tossed it to the side, then grabbed a sandwich and took a bite of the savory roast beef sandwiched between two thick slices of bread.

Good, almost as tender as his mother's. He wondered if she'd had a hand in cooking today's meal. His ma missed being able to cook for the lumber crews, but after arthritis set in, her fingers were too drawn and stiff to do much cooking, other than for herself. All she'd ever known was cooking. They'd travelled all over the south, from lumber camp to lumber camp, his pa logging, his ma working in more camp kitchens than a body could count. He and his brothers had cut their teeth on saw blades and loblolly pines.

"So, what do you think, big brother?" Caleb pressed.

"About what?"

"About Miss Denson. Is she pretty?"

Eli scowled. Oh, she was pretty all right, but she didn't seem to be the type to be interested in a lumberjack. "I don't think we'll be seeing much more of Miss Denson. She's a city girl through and through."

Josiah stabbed a finger at the remaining sandwich. "You gonna eat that?"

"Naw. Go ahead. But you'd better be quick. We've got work to do."

Within minutes, they finished their meal and packed up the basket, set it aside and went back to work. The crew set about stripping the limbs on one side of the tree from top to bottom, then used log rollers to roll the heavy tree over to get to the other side.

Eli grabbed his axe and started swinging at the smaller limbs, and that's when he saw it; a soft, gauzy crocheted shawl nestled on the forest floor. Blue. Like her eyes. He reached for the flimsy material and a vision of Lucy Denson crushed beneath the tree slammed into him. How close she'd come to death. How close they'd both come when he rushed to save her.

He tucked the shawl inside his shirt, the cotton warm against his skin. As he picked up his axe, he took a deep breath and released it slowly, closed his eyes, bowed his head, and offered up a prayer of thankfulness that they'd both been spared.

Chapter 3

B ut I can't."

"Oh, I'm sorry, Lucy." Jack's wife rushed about the outdoor summer kitchen, her brow wrinkled. "With Annabelle sick, I wasn't thinking about your accident. Are you feeling all right?"

"I'm fine. Really." Lucy ducked her head, wishing Maggie would just forget about her near accident. "It's just that I don't know how to fry chicken."

Maggie shoved a bowl of potatoes into her hands. "Well, just peel these potatoes, and I'll take care of the rest."

Lucy set to work, glad of something to do to help. The creak of Mrs. Everett's rocking chair set a frenetic pace as she rocked Maggie's baby, along with the clatter of pots and pans as Maggie prepared supper for the logging crews.

"I'm sorry, child, I should have warned you to be careful." Mrs. Everett's lined face filled with worry. "The woods can be dangerous when the fallers are around."

"It's not your fault, Mrs. Everett." Lucy dipped her head, face flaming. "Any idiot should have known better."

The rocking chair stopped, and a storm cloud gathered on the elderly woman's brow. "Did my son say that?"

"No ma'am." Eli Everett hadn't called her an idiot, but he might as well have. She'd seen the look in his eyes, the one that told her he thought she was a brainless twit who wouldn't know how to get out of the rain—or out of the way of a falling tree.

Mrs. Everett hefted Maggie's colicky baby higher on her shoulder and started rocking again, her foot tilting the rocker back and forth with dizzying speed. "He'd better be glad. I might be old and decrepit, but I'd take a stick to that boy if he said such a thing to a lady."

Lucy ducked her head, hiding a smile. The idea of the tiny, white-haired woman taking a switch to her grown son seemed ludicrous, but the fierce glare in her eyes left no doubt she knew how to give all four of her boys a tongue-lashing they'd never forget if they disobeyed her.

Maggie rushed to the stove and opened the damper. "Oh no, look at the time. The men will be here soon, and

I haven't even cut up the chickens yet. It'll take forever to fry it all."

"Maggie, why don't you make chicken stew or dumplings? It would be faster and would fill those men up in a hurry."

Maggie scrunched up her nose. "Frying chicken for fifteen men was not my idea. But it's Samuel's favorite, and today's their anniversary, so Annabelle wanted fried chicken tonight."

Mrs. Everett grunted. "Just wait until she has two hundred to cook for. She'll change her tune right quick."

Two hundred men? The very thought made Lucy queasy. She peeled faster, wishing she could do more to help, but the sight of raw chicken turned her stomach. She finished the potatoes, wiped her hands, and took a deep breath. Poor Maggie looked as flustered as a swarm of bees after a honeysuckle vine. "Maggie, what else can I do?"

Maggie spared her a glance as she cut up a chicken. "Mix up a batch of cornbread. Use that washtub over there, and triple whatever you're used to making. Hopefully, it'll be enough."

Cornbread. It couldn't be that hard, could it? Lucy grabbed the washtub and searched for the cornmeal. That much she knew.

Mama had always shooed her out whenever she'd ventured into the kitchen, saying her daughter's presence made her nervous. Instead, Lucy had turned her talents toward keeping the house spotless and volunteering on various committees at church. She had a knack for decorating, so she'd been quite busy since she'd finished school. At least until her father had plucked them up and moved them to the backwoods of Mississippi. From the looks of the rough housing the lumberjacks lived in and the simple clapboard church, she didn't expect to find many opportunities to pretty things up around here. She plopped the cornmeal beside the washtub and glanced around. What now?

Her panicked gaze met Mrs. Everett's, and without missing a beat, the elderly woman nodded at a tub on the shelf above her head. "Lucy, there's the lard, right up there. Maggie, where are the eggs?"

And just like that, Mrs. Everett gently guided Lucy through the ingredients needed to mix up the cornbread. Lucy shared a smile with the elderly woman and stirred the grainy mixture, pleased with her efforts. Maybe she could learn to cook after all.

The baby started fussing then let out a howl. Maggie groaned. "Not now, Aaron. Mama's busy."

Mrs. Everett rocked harder, trying to appease the crying child. But to no avail. He just cried harder. "It's no use, Maggie. You might as well go feed him. He's not going to hush until you do."

Maggie looked around the disaster of a kitchen. "But—"

"Go on. Lucy and I can finish up here."

"I'll be right back." Maggie clutched her baby and headed toward the cabin Jack had built at the edge of the clearing, when he'd been courting Maggie almost two years ago.

Lucy stared at the mound of raw chicken, wondering how she'd manage. Gingerly, she reached for a piece of chicken, knowing it wasn't going to cook itself.

"Never you mind about frying chicken, Lucy. Boil it and make dumplings."

Relieved to have someone else in charge, Lucy did as she was told. Soon the chicken was boiling in the water meant for the potatoes. "Now what?"

Mrs. Everett nodded toward the stove. "Turn the damper down and let that grease cool a bit. Fried potatoes go a long way toward filling up a bunch of hungry men." She flexed her arthritic fingers. "I wish I could help, but these stiff hands can barely hold a knife anymore. It's a pitiful thing to be old and useless."

"That's all right, Mrs. Everett. You've been more help than you know."

"Might as well call me Ma. Everybody does." Mrs. Everett rocked and kept Lucy busy for the next hour.

"Check on the cornbread."

"How's the chicken?"

"Stir those peas."

"Don't forget the potatoes."

"Oh no, the potatoes." Lucy grabbed a spatula and a

dishcloth. She moaned. "They're sticking."

"They'll be fine. Close that damper. Yes, that one. Put a little water in the pan and put a lid on. In a few minutes, they'll be fine. And on the next batch, toss 'em with a little flour. That'll keep 'em from sticking."

By the time Maggie returned with Aaron, Lucy had made headway into the mound of fried potatoes, three pones of cornbread sat in the warming oven, and chicken and dumplings simmered over the reservoir on the back of the stove. And per Mrs. Everett's instructions, Lucy had just fished her first batch of doughnut holes out of the grease and sprinkled them with cinnamon and sugar.

Maggie stopped and stared at the kitchen. "I thought you said you couldn't cook."

Lucy grinned, reached over, and hugged Mrs. Everett, leaving a streak of flour on her weathered cheek. "I can't. But Ma Everett can. So between the two of us, we managed to get the job done."

Chapter 4

At the end of the day, Eli and Josiah took a dip in Sipsey Creek, washing off the grime and sweat from a hard day's work. He tossed his knapsack on the bed, and Lucy Denson's crocheted shawl spilled out across the patchwork quilt.

"You coming?" Josiah called out as he hurried out the door and bounded down the steps, toward the tables set up under the lean-to in the shade of the pines.

"Yeah, be right there." Eli walked to the door, fingering the shawl even as he spotted Lucy flitting about the summer kitchen. He shoved the shawl back in his pack. She wouldn't want him flaunting her mishap in front of the other men. He'd give it back to her later.

Minutes later, he stood in line, plate in hand. Maggie

and Lucy ladled chicken and dumplings, fried potatoes, peas, and thick slabs of cornbread on each plate. His stomach rumbled.

"How'd it go today, Everett? Samuel Frazier slapped him on the back. Your crew do okay?"

Eli nodded. "We felled a dozen trees and snaked 'em out to the log road. A couple of real good punkins. Couldn't ask for better."

"Any problems?"

Eli's gaze met Lucy's across the makeshift sideboard, and a becoming blush stole over her cheeks. She lowered her gaze and ladled a helping of dumplings onto Josiah's plate. "Nope. Everything went fine."

"Good to hear."

Eli and Samuel moved up in line. Samuel frowned and looked around. "Where's Annabelle?"

"She wasn't feeling well earlier and went home." Maggie took Samuel's plate, heaped it full of potatoes and peas, then held it out to Lucy for a generous serving of chicken and dumplings. Maggie pushed the plate back at her brother-in-law, a smile playing on her lips. "And here's your supper. You can share with Annabelle, but I doubt she'll be able to eat anything."

Samuel blanched. "What's the matter with her?"

"Maybe you should ask your wife that."

The man hurried away, and Maggie and Lucy filled Eli's plate. At the end of the table, a huge pan of cinnamon and sugarcoated bear sign made his mouth water. He popped one of the doughnuts in his mouth and groaned at the sugary sweetness.

As good as his own mother's.

"Maggie-girl, you and Annabelle outdid yourselves today."

Maggie shrugged. "Wasn't us. With Annabelle sick and Aaron being so fussy, Lucy did most of the cooking today."

"Really?" Eli's gaze snapped to Lucy.

She lifted a pale eyebrow.

Oops, he'd offended her. He grabbed a handful of bear sign and nodded in appreciation. "Tastes a lot like Ma's."

As he searched for a place to sit, he caught the glance Lucy shared with his mother. His mother smiled and nodded, looking happier than he'd seen her in a long time.

Lucy frowned at Eli, who sat hunched over at one of the rough-hewn tables, his attention focused on his plate. He shoveled food into his mouth like he hadn't eaten all week.

She wrinkled her nose. No table manners there. But the other men were eating with just as much gusto, laughing, talking, and devouring their food at an alarming rate. She bit her lip, the sheer abandon they exhibited while eating making her nervous. Where were their table manners? Why, Deotis would never make such a spectacle of himself.

But regardless of the way they were eating, she couldn't help but be pleased they seemed to like her cooking—or Mrs. Everett's, anyway. She'd cooked a meal and nobody pushed their plates away. But could she do it again? The last few hours had passed in a blur, with Mrs. Everett not giving her a minute's rest. *Close the damper. Open the damper. Remove the doughnuts, no, the—bear sign, from the grease. Hurry! Set those dumplings to the side before they scorch. Scorched dumplings weren't fit for a cat to eat,* she'd said.

And on and on. Lucy's head was spinning from the instructions, and she'd never wanted to set foot in a kitchen again.

Until the ravenous logging crew devoured what she'd cooked, scooted back the rough-hewn benches, and lined up for seconds. Even Eli, one of the last to arrive, pushed back from the table, made an end-run around the other men, grabbed a handful of bear sign, and taking his mother's arm, led her away toward a two-room shanty nestled among the trees. As the men wandered away, Maggie scraped the last of the potatoes into a battered metal pan. "Well, that went over well. We'll get things cleaned up and get ready for breakfast."

"Breakfast?"

"Oh, it's nothing like this. Flapjacks and ham, mostly. Sorghum molasses and butter. The men will want to be through eating and in the woods by daylight though, so we have to get cracking mighty early. And if Annabelle is still not feeling well—"

"Daylight?" Lucy squeaked.

What had she gotten herself into?

Chapter 5

A clatter jerked Eli awake and he lay in the darkness, wondering what had stirred him from slumber before the gut-hammer sounded.

His brothers snored in their bunks in the shanty they'd built when they first arrived in Sipsey. They'd added a separate room for their mother, so she could have some privacy. Had his mother gotten out of bed? Fallen, maybe?

He swung his legs out of bed and padded on sock feet toward her room. She was still sleeping soundly. As he turned, he spotted the lantern on in the cook shack. Banging and a softly uttered exclamation drifted across the clearing.

Pulling on his trousers, he stomped into his boots and headed toward the kitchen. He'd grab a cup of coffee and watch the sunrise, then bring his mother a cup back so she could enjoy it in peace while the crews wolfed down breakfast before heading to the woods.

The sight that greeted him at the kitchen brought him up short. Lucy Denson stood in the middle of the shack, a cloud of flour hovering around her. "Lucy?"

She whirled, her blue eyes wide. "Oh, Eli, what am I going to do?"

"What's the matter? Where's Maggie and Annabelle?"

"Annabelle's still not feeling well and Aaron has got the croup. Jack said Maggie would be here as soon as she could, but for me to go ahead and get started."

Eli glanced around the kitchen at the cold stove and the fixings for flapjacks. He rubbed his neck and squinted at Lucy. "Uh, Lucy, have you ever fixed flapjacks before?"

Her eyes filled with tears. "I've never fixed any meal before last night."

"Never?"

She shook her head. "If it hadn't been for your mother's help, I don't know what I would have done."

"I see." And he did see. Those dumplings and the bear sign had tasted just like his mother's cooking. He rubbed his hands together. "Well, the crew will be here anytime, so let's get started."

She held out both hands, warding him off. "Oh, but you can't. It's not your job."

"Doesn't matter. It's got to be done and looks like it's

you and me this morning." Eli hunkered down and opened the firebox on the stove and stirred up the ashes. At least Maggie had banked the fire real good last night. "Do you know how to work the stove?"

"No. Mama wouldn't let me near the kitchen." Even in the dim light cast from the lantern, the misery on Lucy's face was evident. She leaned in close, a look of fierce determination on her face. "I know I'm next to useless in the kitchen, but I'm willing to learn if you'll just show me."

Eli jostled her shoulder. "Hey, don't say that. Anybody who can cook as fine a meal as you did last night, just from Ma's instructions, can learn how to get the stove going in the mornings and whip up a batch of flapjacks."

"You think so?" She sniffed and blinked, her eyelashes fluttered against her cheeks, then swept up to reveal eyes as blue as a clear summer sky. Eli froze, lost in the bottomless pools of her sky-blue eyes.

He cleared his throat and jerked open the damper on the stove. "I do. Now, listen carefully."

Lucy watched every move Eli made. His large work-roughened hands got the stove going, sliced ham, started frying it, then showed her how to mix up a batch of pancakes.

"Flapjacks are about the easiest things in the world to

make. As long as they're not raw or burnt, the men won't care." He plopped some lard on the large griddle and used a spatula to spread it out. He sprinkled water on the flat surface, and it sizzled and splattered. Lucy jumped, but he snagged her around the waist and pulled her back.

"It's not going to hurt you. See, when the water sizzles and dances across the griddle, the stove's just the right temperature. Now, pour your batter. Not much, about the size of a saucer."

Lucy smiled as the circular rounds of batter formed perfectly on the griddle. But the bowl grew heavy, and on her third attempt, she poured way too much. Eli grabbed the bowl and tipped it up, laughing. "Enough. You won't be able to flip that monster over!"

"I'm sorry." One arm wrapped securely around the large bowl, the other clutching the spatula, Lucy rubbed her face against her sleeve, trying to push a wisp of hair off her face. "It's heavy."

Eli reached out and tucked her hair behind her ear. His brown eyes crinkled at the corners, and his gaze shifted and moved lazily across her face. His thumb rubbed softly against her cheek, and she shivered at his touch. "You've got flour on your face."

"I'm—I'm not surprised." Lucy whispered past the lump in her throat. She needed to move away, to put some space between them, but there wasn't much room between the stove and the long sideboard, where they served the meals. She took a shuddering breath, willing her lungs to breathe.

Eli's eyelids fell to half-mast and his gaze dropped to her lips. For a wild moment, Lucy wondered if this big, brawny man who towered over her was going to kiss her. Her heart pounded. He wasn't. . .she didn't. . .

An incessant clanging rent the air and Lucy jumped, nearly losing her grip on the bowl of batter. The men's wake-up call had her turning toward the griddle. "Well," she said, her voice high-pitched from sheer nerves—"the men will be here any minute. What next?"

Eli leaned around her, plucked the spatula from her nerveless fingers and flipped a flapjack over, the batter perfectly browned. "You just flip 'em when they're brown, and that's it. All right?"

Lucy nodded, taking the spatula from him.

Maggie came rushing in, grabbed an apron, and tied it on. "Oh, Lucy, bless you."

"It wasn't—"

Eli touched his fingers to her lips. *"Shh."*

Then winking, he grabbed a cup, poured himself a cup of coffee he'd made, and settled onto one of the benches. "Morning, Maggie."

Chapter 6

Eli sipped his coffee as one by one the men crowded under the lean-to. They jostled for position near the stove and the coffee he'd set to boiling earlier. He frowned. Or were they just getting closer to Lucy? Even Caleb, who didn't even like coffee, stood near the stove.

Every single one of them dwarfed her slender frame as she focused on making flapjacks. Where Maggie rushed about the open area flipping ham and frying potatoes, Lucy stood firmly in front of the griddle, watching the flapjacks as if her life depended on getting them just right.

She eased up a flapjack and peered underneath. Seemingly satisfied they were brown enough, she scooped the cakes up one at a time and piled them on a platter, then carried them to Maggie. Maggie grabbed the huge platter and placed it on the table. "We'll need more."

His lips twitched when Lucy's eyes grew wide. "More?"

Maggie darted away, forking up ham and whipping around so fast it made his head spin. As the men dug into their breakfast, Lucy turned back to the stove and carefully poured out another batch of flapjacks.

Eli shook his head at the precise way she attempted to make each pancake the exact same size, all of them perfectly round, perfectly browned. She'd learn the men didn't care what the food looked like as long as it was reasonably tasty and kept their bellies full until their next meal.

Lucy felt Eli's gaze on her, but kept her attention firmly on the task at hand. She knew she needed to help Maggie with the rest of the meal, but she was afraid she'd burn the flapjacks if she left them unattended. Better to stay at her station than to show how utterly incompetent she was in the kitchen.

Maggie single-handedly kept the men supplied with fried potatoes, ham, coffee, butter, and syrup, while all Lucy could do was cook flapjacks. Her face heated; she pressed her lips together and peeked to see if this latest batch was done. Satisfied they were, she flipped them over. She eyed the pale yellow orbs. They didn't look done enough. Maybe she should flip them back over. Frowning, she studied the pancakes, trying to decide what to do. Was the stove hot enough? Did she need to open the damper? Or add more wood?

Maggie hurried to the stove, the empty platter in her hand. "Those ready?"

Lucy poked at the flapjacks. "I'm not sure."

Maggie grabbed the spatula and deftly flipped one over. "They'll do."

Within seconds, she'd stacked all the flapjacks on the platter and tossed it on the table. Forks stabbed at the golden cakes, ripping them apart as the men grabbed pieces off the platter. They slathered the flapjacks with globs of butter and sorghum molasses and hunkered over them, shoveling the food into their mouths.

Lucy shook her head at the free-for-all as the men devoured the flapjacks, the rest of Maggie's ham, and six pots of coffee. A man with shoulders like an ox stood, reached across the table and picked up the leftover potatoes, dumped them on his plate and poured half a jar of tomato relish on top. He then picked up a fork and started eating without missing a beat.

Someone clanged on the gut-hammer and just as suddenly as they appeared, the men gulped down the last of their coffee and stood, moving away from the kitchen all as one unit. One bench fell over with a thud as they all trooped out. Lucy stared at the mess they'd left. She'd never seen anybody eat like that. Not even last night had been as chaotic. Eli tipped the bench upright and pushed it under the table, and her gaze met his.

He tipped his slouch hat toward her and Maggie then loped away, hoisting himself on the back of one of the log wagons headed toward the woods.

Chapter 7

By the time Uncle Hiram dismissed church Sunday morning and the congregation filed out to enjoy dinner on the ground, Lucy's smile felt frozen in place. They'd moved away eight years ago and, other than Uncle Hiram, her aunts, and her cousins Annabelle and Jack, she didn't remember any of the people who insisted they'd known her from the day she was born.

While her mother carried food from the wagon to the long tables spread out beneath the towering pines, Lucy enlisted her younger cousins to gather wildflowers. As the ladies laid old quilts and sheets on the tables, Lucy placed canning jars filled with flowers on top. The bright-colored flowers brought out the reds, yellows, and blues in the quilts. She stepped back, admiring her handiwork. She eyed the flowers on one of the tables, grabbed a couple out of a jar that was overflowing, and poked them in a skimpy one.

Aunt Eugenia smiled at her from the other side of the table. "I declare, Lucy, you sure do have a way with flowers. Sunday dinner has never looked so inviting. Would you be willing to help decorate for the Independence Day celebration?

"Of course. What did you have in mind?" Lucy helped her aunt arrange the food on the table around the flowers.

"Well, flowers for starters. And the men will build a speaker's platform, so we'll need bunting for that."

"What about fireworks?" Lucy loved the annual fireworks display in Chicago. Another thing she'd miss this summer.

"Oh, none of that." Aunt Eugenia frowned. "Too noisy and scares the animals."

A pity about the fireworks. She loved the patterns and stunning colors they made against the night sky. If she could just transfer all of that sparkle to a crochet pattern. She pictured the explosion in her head. Maybe she could come up with a pattern that would look like fireworks. Red, white, and blue pinwheels, with a bit of a spiral. Stars, maybe. . .

Aunt Eugenia continued to discuss the July Fourth celebration and with an effort Lucy pushed thoughts of crocheting and fireworks to the back of her mind. "Could you make place ribbons for the contests; pies, watermelon eating, canning? That sort of thing. And the men have all kinds of events planned. I'll have to ask Samuel how many so we have enough ribbons."

"Yes, ma'am, I'm sure I can come up with something."

"That's settled, then." Aunt Eugenia smiled at someone behind her. "Ah, Mrs. Everett, good to see you looking so well today."

Lucy turned to find Eli and his mother behind her. The elderly woman reached out to pat her on the arm, a secretive smile playing about her lips. "Been doing more cooking?"

"A little." Lucy's gaze lifted and met Eli's, and a blush stole over her cheeks. Had he told his mother about their early morning cooking class? From the look on his face, she guessed not. She turned back to Mrs. Everett. "How are you feeling, ma'am? I missed seeing you yesterday."

"I'm fine." She flexed her fingers. "My arthritis has been acting up and I think I overdid it the other day. But I do have a recipe I want to share with you. Eli wrote it down for me." She fumbled with the drawstrings on her purse. "Oh, drat it."

Eli plucked the black bag from his mother's fingers and pulled open the drawstring, his work-roughened hands large against the small bag. He extracted a crumpled piece of paper and handed it to Lucy. Their fingers brushed, and she lowered her gaze. "Thank you."

"It's kolache. Such sweet little pastries you've never tasted. I'll be glad to show you how to make them."

"Oh, wonderful." Aunt Eugenia clapped her hands. "You could make these for Independence Day, Lucy. It's always nice to have a new dish or two on the table."

Mrs. Everett leaned close and whispered, "Apricot is Eli's favorite."

Lucy blushed and refused to look at Eli. Had he heard what his mother had said? Instead, she glanced at the piece of paper. Scribbling filled the entire first page and spilled over onto the back. Oh my! "Thank you, ma'am, but I hate to put you to so much trouble."

"It's no trouble, dear. Just let me know if you decide to make them." Mrs. Everett's smile faded, and she patted Lucy on the arm. "Eli, can you help me to my rocker? My legs are getting a mite tired."

Lucy bit her lip in consternation. Had she offended Mrs. Everett by not being more enthusiastic about the recipe? But it looked so complicated! Worry furrowed her brow. She'd have to do something to make it right, starting with making sure she had all the ingredients on hand to try her hand at making kolaches.

Eli leaned against the trunk of a pine tree along the

creek bank, watching the children play in the water. Even some of the older folks had removed their shoes and waded along the edges, cooling off as the day grew hotter.

He grinned as Jack dipped little Aaron's bare feet in the water. Lucy and Maggie laughed as the boy squealed and kicked, splashing water all over Jack. When Maggie and Jack headed back to the wagon with a thoroughly wet child, Lucy's attention focused on the wild roses growing on the bank. She plucked one of the blooms and studied it carefully as she walked toward him, her attention totally captured by the pink bud.

She glanced up and her gaze met his. Her cheeks pinkened to the shade of the flower in her hand. "Oh, I didn't know you were there."

"Hope I didn't startle you." He gestured toward the flower. "What's so fascinating about a wild rose?"

She smiled, a shy, teasing smile, and holding the flower up, twirled it around. "I'm studying it so I can figure out how to crochet flowers that look like this."

"Hmm. I see."

Her brow arched. "Do you?"

He squinted and shook his head. "Not really."

She lifted the edges of her shawl, much like the one he'd found in the woods, except this one was white. He meant to return her other one, but every time he'd reach for it, he'd found an excuse to keep it longer. "See this pattern?

Do you know what this is?"

He shook his head. "I can't say that I do."

"Pinecones."

He peered at the shawl and nodded. "Well, I'll be. That does look like pinecones."

She laughed, the soft tilt of her lips doing funny things to his insides. "I've been studying the way the cones look and finally got the hang of it a couple of days ago. I just finished this last night."

"It's pretty." He snapped his fingers. "Is that why I found a pinecone in our lunch the other day?"

"Probably." She smirked and held out the rest of the shawl. "See this? It's a spider-web pattern."

Eli nodded. Even he could see the resemblance. He quirked an eyebrow at her. "Have you ever seen hoarfrost or the early morning dew on a spider web? It sparkles and shines in the sunlight. Like—" He shrugged. He didn't have words to describe it, but he knew she'd like it. He shifted and looked down at his dusty boots. "There's nothing like it."

"I'd love to see it sometime, but—" she squished up her nose in distaste. "I'm not fond of traipsing around in the woods, looking for spider webs."

"There's really not that much to be afraid of in the woods." He glanced at her and grinned. "Other than having a tree fall on you."

Chapter 8

Lucy placed the last jar of wildflowers on one of the tables and eyed her handiwork. She smiled, wondering if the loggers would notice the sprig of pine needles she'd stuck in the jars for added greenery, or the red-and-white-checked gingham strips she'd tied around the jars for more color.

"What are you doing?"

Lucy turned at the sound of Annabelle's voice. She hurried to her cousin's side and hugged her. "Are you feeling better? I've been worried."

"Much better. Until tomorrow morning, I expect."

"Oh." Lucy held her at arm's length. "Morning sickness?"

Annabelle laughed, a secretive smile on her face, a hand to her middle. "Yes. I think; I hope."

"Oh, Annabelle." Lucy hugged her again. "Have you told Samuel?"

"Yes, last night. It's too early to know for sure, but Mama thinks so, too." She glanced around. "So, what are you doing with all these wildflowers?"

Lucy shrugged. "I thought I'd try to spruce things up a bit. The flowers are pretty, and I thought the men might enjoy them."

Annabelle shook her head as she tied on an apron. "Well, don't be surprised if they don't even notice."

The men lined up for supper as calm as could be. No pushing and shoving. They even removed their caps. They took their places at the tables, eating quietly and without their usual rowdy behavior. Annabelle leaned close to Lucy and whispered, "I wouldn't have believed it if I hadn't seen it. Even Ox is showing some table manners. Amazing."

Lucy stood at the sideboard, watching the men eat. Some of them talked among themselves, while the others ate silently, not even glancing up from their plates. She caught Eli's gaze and he gave her a tiny smile. A few of the men came back for seconds, and Lucy ladled hash onto their plates. Ox didn't move, but she noticed him eyeing his empty plate and the tomato relish at the end of the table.

Suddenly, it dawned on Lucy that she'd made a big mistake. The flowers made the men nervous. She tucked the pan of hash under her arm and hurried over to the tables. "More hash, Mr. Ox?"

"Why, thank ye, Miss Lucy." The big man smiled up at her and held out his plate.

She gave him two big helpings then continued to make the rounds, ladling hash on empty plates. The hum of conversation grew but didn't get to the deafening level it had been during previous meals. As soon as the men finished eating, they got up from her pretty table, careful not to jostle anything or overturn the mason jars. They didn't linger over coffee and dessert as they usually did. Respectfully, they thanked her, Maggie, and Annabelle for the meal before walking away.

But something was lacking.

And Lucy knew exactly what it was.

She'd tried to bring a bit of cheer to the table with her girly decorations but had only succeeded in tamping down the men's jovial spirit. Supper was a time for them to relax and enjoy each other's company after a hard day in the woods.

And she'd ruined it for them.

Eli nursed his coffee and watched the men wander away.

Lucy slid onto the bench across from him with a plate of hash, but she didn't eat. Instead, she caught his gaze, looking miserable. "Looks like I messed up again."

Eli smiled at her through the gathering twilight. "How so?"

She reached out and flicked the tips of her fingers at the wildflowers. "I thought the men would appreciate the flowers, but they just made them uncomfortable. I should have left well enough alone."

Eli leaned forward and rested his elbows on the table. "Ah, Lucy, they did appreciate them. And it wasn't the flowers, but the thought of messing up your pretty table that made them nervous. And, I imagine it made some of them think of home, of their mama's table, of family."

She stabbed her fork at her hash, her lip turned down in a mulish pout. "Well, I liked the men better the way they were."

He chuckled. "And how's that?"

"When they came rushing in here, pushing and shoving to be first in line, demanding seconds, and—"

"Licking their plates clean?"

"Well, maybe not that." She winced then shook her head.

"Does the fact that they don't have good table manners bother you?"

"Well, yes. No." She took a dainty bite of hash and wiped her mouth with a clean napkin. "But they proved they could act civilized if they wanted to."

Eli dipped his head and stared down at his coffee

cup. He seriously doubted today's display of manners from the men would be good enough for polite society. Crumbling cornbread into your soup with your fingers and reaching across the table to grab whatever you needed wouldn't endear them to any woman's sense of propriety. "Civilized enough for Chicago's crusty upper class?"

A small laugh escaped her. "I wouldn't know how the upper class lives."

He motioned at the open-air summer kitchen, the rough-cut boards resting on saw horses, the hard-packed dirt floor. "I imagine this is a long way from what you're used to, regardless."

"Some." She shrugged. "In Chicago, Mama had dinner on the table promptly at six. And Papa better not be late or she was not happy."

"At least your pa gets home on time, now that he's working for Jack and Samuel."

"Last Christmas, I was invited to a Christmas ball by a. . ." Was that a blush that stole over her cheeks? ". . .a friend, and I felt a bit uncomfortable. Crystal chandeliers and silver spoons. I'd never seen so much food. And it was served in courses. Soup first, then fish, then—oh, I don't remember what came next, but it was wonderful. I sat across from one of the curators from the Newberry Library, and he talked about his travels abroad to secure books for the library. He'd been to Rome, London, and *Paris*. And there were flowers everywhere. The centerpiece was so big I couldn't even see over it. Can you imagine?"

Her gaze met his, shining from the memory of her fancy feast and even fancier dinner conversation. He wouldn't know a polite conversation if it hit him over the head, and he was still in the woods at six.

"Nope. I can't even picture such a thing." He glanced at the rough tables and Lucy's attempts to pretty the place up. A far cry from silver and crystal. "But it couldn't be any prettier than the wildflowers you picked for the men. Even if they didn't say anything, they appreciated your thoughtfulness."

"Why, thank you, Eli. What a sweet thing to say." She fingered the jar of wildflowers between them. "But it doesn't matter. There aren't going to be any more flowers, not here at least. The men should be able to enjoy their meal without worrying about toppling over a jar of flowers."

Her gaze lifted and captured his as she pushed the jar of flowers toward him. "Would you take these to your mother? I think she'd enjoy them, and I would hate to throw them out."

Eli reached out, his hand capturing hers against the coolness of the jar. He knew he should pull back, but he didn't want to let go, not yet. Slowly, he rubbed his thumb across the knuckles on the back of her hand. Her smile slipped and she lowered her gaze, but she didn't pull away.

"Lucy, got a letter for you today." Samuel strode into the circle of light cast by the lanterns. Lucy slipped her hand away, and Eli slid the jar of flowers toward him as if nothing had happened. But his heart thudded inside his chest like a runaway mule, just from touching her hand. Samuel handed Lucy her letter. "From some feller up in Chicago, named Deotis Reichart."

Eli took a sip of his cold coffee and scowled behind the rim of his cup. Was Deotis Reichart the friend who'd invited her to the fancy dinner party? He'd bet his best crosscut saw on it.

Chapter 9

"Come on, I want to show you something."

Lucy looked up from the flapjack batter she'd just mixed up. The gut-hammer hadn't even sounded, and Eli stood in the early morning light, his dark eyes shining with excitement. Lucy eyed the big bowl of batter, frowning. "I can't right now. Can't it wait until later?"

"Nope. It'll be gone."

Annabelle took the bowl and shooed her away even as Lucy spotted Maggie hurrying across the yard toward the kitchen. "Go on. I think Maggie and I can handle everything for a while."

Eli grabbed her hand and led her away from the cook shack, down the road, past the sawmill toward Sipsey. A slight misty rain had fallen during the night, just enough to settle the dust on the roads. Lucy hurried to keep up with Eli. "Where are we going?"

"You'll see."

The sun rose behind them, bathing the grass and trees in early morning light. A half mile down the road, Eli paused and walked into a field of wildflowers, still damp with dew. He pointed. "Look."

Lucy stood on the log road, her gaze following his line of sight. There, suspended between two trees, was a spider web, the silky strands covered with millions of tiny raindrops. They watched in silence as the sun rose, shining its bright light on the web. The water droplets sparkled and shone in the light, like row upon row of delicate pearls. Lucy gasped in delight and pressed her hands together. "Oh, Eli, it's spectacular."

"There's more." He squatted and pointed at the wildflowers. Lucy moved, her skirts swishing through the damp grass, but she barely noticed. She crouched by Eli's side, her attention focused on the beauty in front of her. Small cobwebs connected the flowers, tatting them together much like she tatted lace. Dew clung to the webs, the flowers, the green leaves. As her gaze took in the ethereal beauty, something miraculous happened. The sunlight hit one of the drops of dew at the perfect angle and reflected the flowers in the droplet.

Lucy clutched Eli's arm and whispered, "Look at that."

As the sun rose higher, the magical moment slipped

away. The spider web no longer sparkled, the drops of dew started to dissipate. The flowers no longer sparkled like jewels, but Lucy still felt the awe of what she'd seen.

Eli stood, pulling her with him. Lucy shaded her eyes and looked up at him. "Thank you. That was one of the most beautiful sights I've ever seen."

His eyes met and held hers, a crooked smile twisting his mouth. "Prettier than the chandeliers in Chicago?"

She glanced around the meadow, God's handiwork still fresh and clear in her mind's eye. She nodded. "Yes, even prettier than that."

Chapter 10

I learned how to make kolaches from a Czech immigrant in one of the lumber camps over in Louisiana," Mrs. Everett said.

Lucy bit her lip and concentrated on mixing the dough for the pastry, just as she'd been instructed. They made cream cheese, apricot, and blueberry, even though Mrs. Everett lamented not having any poppy seeds, a common staple in the ones the Czech cook had made. Lucy slid the pastries into the oven just as Maggie appeared with Aaron in tow.

"Hand me that sweet baby." Mrs. Everett snuggled Aaron against her and kissed his cheek as she rocked him back and forth.

Maggie sniffed appreciatively. "Hmmm, something smells good."

"Kolaches. They taste like doughnuts, but much better." Mrs. Everett smiled at Lucy. "It's Lucy's contribution to the Independence Day celebration."

"I'm not sure how they're going to turn out. I had a bit of trouble with the dough." Lucy turned at the sound of a wagon lumbering down the road toward them. "Oh, there's Papa with the decorations. But the kolaches—"

"They'll be fine." Maggie tied on an apron. "You go on ahead and take care of making everything look pretty. That is one chore I have no talent for."

"Are you sure?"

"Definitely. Now *shoo.* I've got a chicken potpie to make, and Mrs. Everett is going to help me. You're not the only one who's taking lessons from her."

Mrs. Everett chuckled.

Lucy took off her apron and fluffed her skirt. She'd worn her prettiest dress for today's festivities. She smoothed her hair back, grabbed her bonnet, and kissed Mrs. Everett on the cheek. "Thank you," she whispered.

"No. Thank you. It makes me happy that you young ones are learning how to cook these dishes." She smiled, her eyes twinkling. "You know good victuals are the way to a man's heart, don't you?"

Lucy's face flamed. "So they say."

Once Eugenia got it in her head that it was going to rain on

Independence Day, what started out as a simple speaker's platform ended up being a major project.

Eli pounded in a nail then wiped his brow. "I sure hope she's right about that rain, because it's going to be a scorcher."

"Aunt Eugenia's never wrong." Samuel laughed and slapped him on the back. "Stick around and you'll find out soon enough."

Eli, with Samuel's and Josiah's help, put the finishing touches on the roof just as Lucy and her father pulled up in the wagon.

Mr. Denson waved him over. "Eli, help me out with all this froufrou Lucy's got here. There's enough red, white, and blue bunting to drape the entire town of Union, let alone Sipsey."

"Oh hush, Papa!" Lucy laughed and let Eli lift her to the ground. A jolt of awareness shot through him at the feel of her soft fingers resting against his arm. Such a simple touch, and so brief, but one he couldn't ignore.

Pulling his attention to the job at hand, Eli helped unload boxes of bunting, wildflowers, and fruit jars, wondering what she intended to do with it all, but knowing she had a plan. As soon as the wagon was unloaded, Mr. Denson pulled himself back into the seat. "I'd better get back to the house. I've got orders from Mrs. Denson to help her load up all her food. You think Lucy has a pile of decorations. Wait until you see all the food my wife's cooked."

"Josiah, get over here and help with this stuff." Eli picked up a box of bunting. "Where do you want this?"

"The bunting goes to the speaker's platform. The tablecloths and flowers on the tables, of course."

Josiah hefted a box, and he and Lucy headed toward the tables. Eli frowned at the colorful bunting in his hands, trying to figure out where Lucy wanted it. He tried to remember how it was hung in years past, but he'd never helped decorate before. What did women want with all these notions anyway?

A few good speeches, a horse race or two, pole climbing, shooting anvils, and all the fried chicken a man could want made the day plenty exciting.

"Not that way." Lucy took the bunting from him and shook it out, the vibrant colors fluttering as she snapped them in the air. "Like this."

She held one end of the bunting while he secured the other end. Then he took hers, but before he could attach it, she stopped him. "No, wait. It needs to be little higher."

Eli bit back a grin and moved the bunting. "Here?"

"Too high. Down a bit." She tipped her head sideways, considering. "There. Perfect."

She fluffed out the bunting, making sure the folds fell just so, then stepped back and sighed. "Doesn't it look pretty?"

Pretty described the happy glow on her face. "Yes ma'am. It looks real nice."

A commotion from the other side of the clearing drew his gaze. Josiah and the lumberjacks hoisted a ninety-foot pole into the air and let it drop with a resounding *thud* into a hole in the ground. A red bandana fluttered from the top.

Lucy eyed the pole that rose to a dizzying height. "What's that for?"

"Pole-climbing event."

"Pole climbing?" Her mouth fell open and she turned her gaze on him. "You climb that pole—all the way to the top?"

Eli laughed. "Yes ma'am."

"It looks dangerous."

"It is. But we do it all the time, so we're good at it." Eli moved closer, his gaze devouring hers. "Are you worried?"

"Of course." She gave him a nervous smile and flicked her gaze away. "Who wouldn't be?"

Lucy couldn't remember even one point from the rousing political speeches. She barely tasted the picnic lunch and accepted congratulations on her kolaches without really registering any of it.

She was too worried about those two poles towering at the edge of the clearing. Her heart pounded at the very thought of anyone attempting to climb such a thing. What was Eli thinking? All too soon, the speeches were over and the crowd hurried to witness the friendly games between the lumberjacks.

The men lined up and threw axes at a wooden target that spanned at least four foot across. The axes whirred through the air, end over end, to embed with solid thuds in the target. She watched nervously as Eli stepped up and toed the line, his gaze intent on the target. Her heart thumped in her chest as he hefted the axe over his head with both hands, set his stance, and tossed it. The crowd cheered as the axe stuck true. Samuel stepped up to the line and tossed, also hitting the target. Back and forth, they competed, the scores tied. Lucy couldn't really tell how Jack could keep score, but somehow he did. And she knew enough about competition to know if one of them hit a bull's-eye, he'd win.

Samuel made a throw and hit the target a bit off center. Jack called out the score. "Come on, Eli, you can do this. You need a bull's-eye to win."

Eli stepped up. He threw the axe and it landed in the middle of the target. The crowd erupted in cheers. Lucy couldn't hold back her grin; she clapped along with everyone else.

Annabelle leaned over. "Well, I can see where your loyalties are."

Lucy's cheeks flamed, and she laughed to cover her embarrassment. "What do you mean?"

"Oh, it's quite obvious." She nodded toward Eli. "He's

quite handsome. A bit rough around the edges, maybe. Nothing like your Mr. Reichart back in Chicago, from what you've said."

"He's not my Mr. Reichart." Lucy squirmed.

Josiah and another man stepped up to try their hand with the axe, drawing Annabelle's gaze back to the games. "But you'd like him to be. Has he written to you?"

"Yes." Lucy caught a glimpse of Eli's broad shoulders as he stood among the men, his brawny arms crossed as he watched the competition. When Josiah's axe hit the target, a wide grin split his face, and he whistled and clapped for his brother.

"And. . ." Annabelle jostled her shoulder, letting her words trail off.

Lucy blinked, turning her full attention on her cousin. "And what?"

Annabelle laughed. "And what did Mr. Reichart say in his letter?"

"He told me about the summer walks in the park, the church picnics, and the latest collection of books on display at the Newberry." Lucy took a deep breath. "And he mentioned that he would like to keep up our correspondence if I was willing."

"And are you? Willing, I mean?"

Lucy's gaze sought out Eli, who took his place with Josiah for the final round. Deotis and Eli were worlds apart. Deotis spent his days clerking in his uncle's warehouse, working his way up through the ranks with plans to take over some day. He dressed in a suit, and at the end of the day, took a stroll through the park before joining his family for dinner, promptly at six. When he'd invited her to the Christmas ball, Lucy had felt like Cinderella at the palace, amid all the glitz and glitter.

Eli threw his axe and hit the bull's-eye. He lifted a fist high in victory and turned, his dark brown gaze catching hers. A smile wreathed his rugged face, and her heart tipped as dangerously as one of those axes flipping through the air, straight toward its target.

She'd thought Deotis and the world he lived in was what she wanted, but now she wasn't so sure. Without taking her gaze off Eli, she whispered, "I don't know."

Chapter 11

Eli gripped the rope and anchored his calked boot into the sides of the pole, ready for the signal to start. He spotted Lucy standing at the edge of the crowd, her fist pressed to her mouth, looking worried.

Before he even realized what he'd done, he winked at her. Her eyes widened, and she looked away, looking flustered. Like an overheated steam engine, Eli's chest nearly exploded from the adrenaline rush her reaction gave him. Maybe that Deotis feller didn't mean anything to her after all.

"Ready?" Samuel called out. "On the count of three. One, two, three!"

Eli pushed off the ground and slapped his left boot into the pole, feeling the spikes grip the trunk. Left foot, right foot, upward, and onward. As he flicked the rope higher on the pole and concentrated on his rhythm all the way to the top, he couldn't help but think about Lucy. He wanted to make her proud, but would the life of a lumberjack, moving from logging camp to logging camp be enough for her? He'd seen the toll that kind of life had taken on his mother. After his pa had died, he and his brothers had taken care of her. They'd still drug her from camp to camp, and she'd never had a place to call her own, but she never complained. Maybe it was time she settled down.

By the time he reached the top of the pole and grabbed the red bandana off the top, he'd made up his mind. He'd talk to his brothers about finding a plot of land for their mother. They'd build her a sturdy cabin, and even if they had to go far afield to provide for her, their mother would have a home. They could come back here, back to Sipsey.

Close to Lucy.

He headed down, lowering the rope, dropping to the ground as fast as he could. The prize money for today's event would go a long way toward helping fulfill his dream for his mother and a family of his own some day.

No more than ten feet off the ground, his gaze caught Lucy's, and he faltered. Next thing he knew, he'd lost his grip and felt himself falling. Somehow he managed to jerk his spiked boots out of the pole and pinwheel his arms to slow his descent. He tucked his knees and hit the ground in a roll, hoping to lessen the impact. It didn't help. He hit the ground with a *thud*, rolled over onto his back, the wind knocked out of him. So much for an impressive finish.

"Eli?"

He opened his eyes. Lucy hovered over him, her face as white as her starched shirtwaist. Her trembling hand rested against his flannel shirt, her warm palm covered his heart. He squeezed her hand and winked.

Everyone crowded around, and Lucy eased out of the way as Eli's brothers brushed past her to help him to his feet. Her gaze met Annabelle's and her cousin grinned. Heat swooshed over Lucy—everyone in Sipsey Creek had seen her unladylike rush to Eli's side.

Annabelle, apparently taking pity on her, snagged her arm and led her toward the tables. "Are there any of those pastries left? I've been hankering for some all afternoon. You're going to have to share the recipe with me."

"It's. . ." Lucy couldn't tear her gaze from Eli as he limped away. "It's Mrs. Everett's recipe. I'm sure she'd be glad to give it to you."

Annabelle bit into a blueberry-topped kolache, closed her eyes, and groaned. "That is so good." Grinning, she reached for a second pastry. "And since I'm eating for two, I'll have another one."

The threat of rain became a reality as the clouds rolled in and women started gathering pots and pans, baskets and blankets. They corralled their husbands and children to carry everything to the waiting wagons. Good-byes and hugs were passed around, and everyone hurried to beat the rain. Even though the festivities had been cut short, the promise of rain was welcome in the hot, dry season.

Lucy grabbed her basket of kolaches and headed toward the speaker's platform. She needed to remove all the bunting before the rain set in. As she untied the first piece, Eli limped toward her. She winced at the look of pain on his face.

"Are you hurt?"

"Mostly my pride." He nodded at the bunting fluttering in the wind. "Need some help?"

"If you don't mind. I don't want the bunting to get wet. We can use it next year."

A funny look crossed his face, but he didn't say anything.

Lucy folded the red, white, and blue cloth. "What did I say?"

He removed another section of bunting and handed it to her. "I wasn't sure if you planned to be here next year."

"Papa seems determined to stay." She folded the cloth without looking at him then tucked it into the box. The sky darkened and a few drops of rain splattered against her cheeks. "We'd better hurry."

Eli and Lucy jerked the last of the bunting off the railings and bounded up the steps as the storm clouds bore down on them. The downpour cocooned them in their own little world while everyone else sought shelter in the church.

Eli leaned against one of the rough posts, his gaze heavy lidded as he watched her. "I wasn't asking about your pa."

"I know."

He straightened and stepped closer, his dark eyes searching hers. Lucy clutched an armful of bunting, her heart pounding at his nearness. The small platform was just big enough for one speaker to engage the crowd; certainly not big enough for the two of them, especially when she was so aware of Eli's presence.

He tucked a strand of hair behind her ear and his fingers slid down the shell of her ear, his palm cupping her jaw. The rain slapping against the roof picked up its tempo, keeping time with her runaway heart.

Without another word, Eli leaned in and captured her lips with his, his kiss sending shivers of delight racing through her veins, exploding in her heart. She only *thought* she'd missed the annual fireworks display in Chicago.

Funny, she hadn't missed a thing.

Chapter 12

The gut-hammer gonged, but it didn't matter. Eli hadn't slept enough to amount to anything. He sat on his bed and fingered Lucy's shawl, the soft, gauzy material sliding through his fingers like silk.

Soft, dainty, and pretty, like her.

How could he expect her to choose him over that man in Chicago? What woman would pick an itinerant lumberjack who didn't even own a home over an educated man set to inherit his uncle's business?

He scowled. And did he want her to choose him?

Well, if the fact that the taste of her lips had broadsided him with the force of a widow-maker had anything to do with it, he did. He'd tossed and turned all night, worrying what he was going to do about his feelings for

Lucy. He loved her. He knew that, without a doubt, and he could barely stand the thought of her heading back to Chicago and marrying another man. But all he had to offer was a lifetime of hardship, picking up and moving all the time, never knowing where they'd be from one year to the next. He'd be sentencing her to the very life his mother had lived; one of constant toil and moving and nothing to show for it in the end. He tossed the shawl on the rumpled quilt beside him and dropped his head into his hands. His heart told him one thing, but his head another.

He froze at the sound of the soft, gentle rustle of his mother's slippers as she shuffled into the room. She paused next to him, one hand on his shoulder.

"That's a mighty pretty shawl, son." She sat on the bed beside him and picked it up. "I'm guessing this is Lucy's. I won't even begin to speculate how you ended up with it."

Eli lifted his head and blew out a long, slow breath. "She lost it the day the tree almost fell on her."

"Ah, I see. And yet, you still have it."

He shrugged. "The time hasn't been right to give it back."

"And now you're not sure you want to."

He clenched his hands together and stared at the wall. "I'm no good for her, Ma. She deserves better than to be dragged all over the country from lumber camp to lumber camp, from shanty to shanty with no place to call home. That's no kind of life for a woman."

His mother grasped his chin, turned him to face her. Fire burned in her dark eyes. "It isn't?"

Eli knew better than to answer, and he also knew his mother was about to give him a piece of her mind.

"Eli, when you boys were coming along, I spent winters with your grandmother in Alabama, but after the babies stopped coming, I told your father I'd rather be with him year-round, and that was that. I spent my life following your father from camp to camp. It was a good life for all of us, and it was what I wanted, not just your pa. We never had much, but we had each other, and we were happy. If I had it to do over again, I'd do it."

"It was fine when you were younger, but now you need a place to live out your life, not worry about where you're going to lay your head next month, next year."

"Oh, I don't worry about the future. I know you and your brothers will take care of me."

"But have you thought about settling down? Would you, if—if we found you a place?"

"I would if it was somewhere you and your brothers could visit often." Her eyes twinkled. "Maybe Sipsey is just the right place."

He shook his head, his gaze on the shawl in her hands. "I don't know, Ma. I'd thought it might be, but I just don't know anymore."

The gut-hammer gonged the second time, and Eli heaved himself off the bed.

His mother frowned up at him. "You missed breakfast."

"I'm not hungry." He patted her shoulder and kissed her on the forehead. He fingered the shawl. "Would you see that Lucy gets this?"

Eli trudged from the shanty to the log wagon that would take him into the woods. Was he still limping? Lucy wasn't sure, but it looked like he might be.

He'd hurt himself yesterday. She knew it. That's why he hadn't come to breakfast this morning. She wanted to run to him and ask how he was feeling, but there was no time. The wagon was already in motion. He lifted his head, his gaze meeting and holding hers as the wagon trundled past. He looked plumb sick.

Lucy frowned, worry filling her thoughts. She wiped her hands on her apron and called over her shoulder to Annabelle and Maggie, "I'll be right back."

She hurried across the yard to the shanty and knocked on the door. Ma Everett opened it on the first knock, a look of surprise on her face. "Oh, good morning, Lucy. I didn't expect to see you so early."

"Yes ma'am. Uh, no ma'am." Lucy glanced in the direction the wagon had gone. "Um, it's Eli. He missed

166

breakfast, and I was worried about him. He did hurt himself yesterday, didn't he? Don't you think he needs to go see a doctor?"

Ma Everett shook her head. "No, child, he's fine. Probably a tad stiff and sore, but he'll be all right."

Lucy frowned. "Then why did he skip breakfast?"

Ma Everett walked onto the porch and sat in one of the rockers, patted the other one. "Sit."

Confused at the odd request, Lucy did as she asked, noticing for the first time the material bundled in Ma Everett's lap. It looked like—Ma Everett held out the shawl.

Lucy took it and shook it out. "Where did you find my shawl?"

"I didn't. Eli did. The day the tree almost fell on you."

Remembering the day Eli had rescued her, Lucy wasn't surprised to see the multitude of snags in the yarn. She should have known better than to wear such a delicate shawl in the woods. And Eli had kept it. But why? She shook her head. "I don't understand."

Ma Everett set her rocker in motion, the gentle movement settling Lucy's thoughts. "There's more than one kind of sick. There's sick in the body, sick in the head, and then there's heartsick." She leaned over and tapped the shawl. "Eli is heartsick."

Lucy's heart pounded against her ribcage. What did Ma Everett mean? She wanted to ask, but couldn't speak past the lump of fear in her throat. She bit her lip and waited.

"Eli's got it in his head that he's not good enough for you." Mrs. Everett's eyes twinkled. "And if you care for him, you'll just have to convince him he's wrong."

Chapter 13

Snaking logs kept Eli busy, and staying busy kept his mind off Lucy.

Or at least it should have. But it didn't. He'd worked in logging long enough he didn't have to think about it too much, even though he knew the dangers of not having his mind on his work.

He walked to the side of the log and slapped the reins against the mules' backs, urging them forward across the ground, slick from yesterday's rain. Josiah had gone on ahead with a log of his own.

As soon as the ground leveled out and the hauling got easier, his thoughts eased right back to yesterday and Lucy. He'd give anything to go back to the hard day's work of two days ago and erase Independence Day from his mind.

Erase the taste of Lucy's kiss, the feel of her in his arms. But it was too late. Her touch was branded into his brain and there was no erasing it.

No, he couldn't undo yesterday, but he could make sure it didn't happen again. He'd pick up his pay tonight and be gone by morning. With him out of the way, Lucy would see that Reichart was the man for her, the man who could offer her the kind of life she'd always dreamed of. The kind he never could.

The mules dipped into an incline and started dragging the log downhill, around a bend. But when they turned to follow the bend, the log began to roll. Eli sidestepped but his boot caught on an exposed root. Even as he fell, he knew he wasn't going to get out of the way in time. The log slammed into him, rolled on top of his legs, and pinned him in place.

He gritted his teeth against the log's weight, praying his legs weren't crushed.

Maybe Josiah was still within hearing range. He yelled for help, but the mules jumped and jerked the log, grinding against his leg even more. Groaning, he lay back against the ground, silent. Somebody would come along shortly. They had to.

Nothing to do, but wait. And pray.

Chapter 14

Fighting back tears of frustration, Lucy concentrated on scrubbing the mound of pots and pans. Around her, Maggie and Annabelle tidied up the cook shack, chatting and laughing.

Eli thought he wasn't good enough for her? She scrubbed harder. He'd probably weighed her, and found *her* wanting instead. She could barely cook, other than what his mother had taught her. And, unlike Maggie and Annabelle, living in Chicago hadn't prepared her for life as a lumberjack's wife. All she seemed good at was decorating, flower arranging, crocheting, and tatting lace.

None of her skills were important around a logging camp, where the work was hard, the hours long, and the men worked from sunup to sundown. . . .and the women even longer. Where dainty shawls and pretty flowers were reserved for Sunday dinners. . .if at all.

She sniffed. In his last letter, Deotis had hinted he might like to visit, come Christmas. A man didn't travel all the way from Chicago to Mississippi just to see the scenery. If she expressed interest, she'd be giving him permission to take their correspondence a step further.

A month ago, she would have been overjoyed. Now, she was just plain-out miserable. Her gaze fell on the blue shawl draped across the back of a chair. Why had Eli kept her shawl but given it to his mother to return to her, the very day after he'd kissed her?

Oh, Eli.

She'd given her heart to a lumberjack, and he'd tossed it back with the same precision he'd toss an axe at a target. And from the pain in her chest, he'd hit the bull's-eye.

Annabelle handed her a stack of plates, a frown of concern on her face. "Are you all right?"

Lucy nodded, her heart too battered to talk about it. "I'm fine—"

Pounding hooves shattered the morning stillness. The women rushed to the edge of the summer kitchen's yard just as one of the draft horses raced into view; Josiah rode on the animal's bare back. He barely slacked up. "There's been an accident. I'm going for the doctor."

"Who?" Annabelle yelled after him as he flew past.

"Eli."

Chapter 15

Lucy ran down the log road, still muddy from yesterday's rain, fear threatening to overwhelm her.

Eli was hurt, maybe dying.

No, he couldn't die. She loved him. She wanted to spend the rest of her life with him. She'd learn to cook. She'd learn to love the woods. She'd learn to not be afraid of snakes and spiders, and dirt and decaying leaves in the forest. She'd learn to endure the gnats and the mosquitoes. Whatever it took, she'd do it.

Mud clung to her shoes, the hem of her skirt, but she ignored the mud and the limbs that reached out and snatched at her hair and her shirtwaist as she searched for the logging crew. She came to a fork. What direction had they taken this morning? Log roads crisscrossed the pine forest, and the men could have gone in any direction.

Please, Lord, show me the way.

She heard the jingle of harnesses deep in the woods to her right, and left the road, running toward the sound, her skirts held high. She stumbled over a root and went flying, landing on the ground with a soft *oomph*. Biting back a sob, she scrambled to her feet and kept going. She had to get to Eli.

In the distance, she spotted the wagon, easing down the rutted log road, Samuel on the seat, more men in the back, several walking behind, quiet as death. Her heart lurched.

She saw her cousin Jack and called out to him. Jack turned and hurried to her side.

"Lucy? What are doing here?"

"Josiah said Eli's been hurt." She clutched his arm. "Is he— Is he—"

"He's going to be fine. His leg might be broke though. The doctor—"

Lucy wilted against him, and Jack patted her arm. Samuel pulled back on the reins at Jack's whistle. Jack led her to the wagon, and she barely noticed when he motioned for the other men to hop out. She had eyes only for Eli.

Jack helped her into the wagon, and she scrambled to where Eli lay against its hard-planked bed, his dark hair sweat-stained in the summer heat, his clothes dirty and coated with mud. Lucy cradled his head in her lap. Fingers shaking, she pushed his hair back from his face and smoothed his furrowed brow. "Eli?"

His eyes opened. He gave her a lopsided smile, the most beautiful sight she'd ever seen. "Lucy."

He groaned when the wagon started up again, tossing him from side to side.

"*Shh.* We'll be out of the woods soon." She leaned down and clutched him to her, trying to ease the jolting, but it was no use. "Where does it hurt?"

He grimaced, but didn't answer. Instead he stared at her so long that her cheeks burned. Then a grin tilted up one side of his mouth, and he captured her hand against his chest, right above his heart. "Here."

Her own heart thudded against her chest at the way his dark gaze caught and held hers. "Did the tree fall on your chest?" she whispered.

"The tree fell on my leg, but it's nothing to the pain in here if"—he grimaced and took a deep breath—"if you decide to go back to Chicago."

"I'm not going anywhere." She brushed his hair away from his forehead, her gaze caressing his face. "Eli Everett, will you marry me?"

"What about your city boy, crystal chandeliers, pretty flowers, and dinner at six?" But even as he questioned her, he caressed her face with the tips of his fingers.

"Who needs hothouse flowers when God clothes the lilies of the field in all His glory, or chandeliers when He uses the morning dew to string pearls on a spider web, and"—Lucy leaned in and whispered against his lips—"who needs a city boy when I've got a lumberjack?"

Award-winning author Pam Hillman, a country girl at heart, writes inspirational fiction set in the turbulent times of the American West and the Gilded Age. She lives with her family in Mississippi. Contact Pam at her website: www.pamhillman.com.

The Summer Harvest Bride

Maureen Lang

For Neil, always my hero.

Chapter 1

Morning, Sally," greeted Mrs. Gibbons as Sally Hobson stepped into the dry goods store. "You just missed Willis. He came in for a packet of pipe tobacco for the mayor not ten minutes ago."

Sally held up the basket of eggs she'd brought to sell, suppressing an inward groan. But why shouldn't Mrs. Gibbons assume she wanted to see Willis at every opportunity? The entire town began linking them together since last year's harvest celebration when Willis had claimed her for nearly every dance. Catching the eye of the mayor's son was considered quite a coup among the young ladies Sally's age.

"I brought our eggs, Mrs. Gibbons."

The storekeeper's wife welcomed the basket at the counter, pulling her cashbox from a shelf underneath. "Did you hear about the newcomers?"

Sally shook her head then waited as Mrs. Gibbons counted the two-dozen eggs.

"Heard tell there's a gang of 'em all in one family. Boys as big as David's Goliath, every last one of them, all fresh from some town back East."

Sally looked toward the window, glad she hadn't seen them and hoping to avoid such a sight on her way back home, just outside of town. Having lived in Chicago, she'd learned to avoid bullies and didn't welcome a pack of them here in the peaceful, quiet town of Finchville.

"They were spotted down by the spring this morning, measuring and counting off steps to who-knows-what. Now they're here in town. One of 'em came in here and invited everyone out to the town pump to hear some kind of idea that's supposed to benefit everybody. Imagine that! Don't even live here, and they're snooping around; then inviting all of us out."

"What sort of benefit?"

"Didn't say." Mrs. Gibbons handed Sally a few coins for the eggs. "Why don't you run on over and see what it's all about? Mr. Gibbons is already there, and you'll probably see Willis, too."

Sally pocketed the money and nodded, although she wasn't sure about following Mrs. Gibbons's suggestion. No one in her family had been gladder than Sally to leave the ever-growing swarm of people in Chicago. She'd rejoiced when Father announced his intention to take up farming on the Illinois prairie in Finchville. The little town sat on the main road between Chicago and Iowa, in the middle of one of the few areas that included a forest, river, and rolling hills on the otherwise flat but fertile prairie.

Still, it did stir curiosity for a group of strangers to gather the entire town together. Wasting everybody's time wasn't likely to inspire many friendships, if they planned to stay. The farmers around town had only one thing on their mind this time of year: planting. The fields were too wet after a late snowmelt and early spring rains, but the land would soon be ready to enfold the seeds of this year's crops.

She stepped outside, wondering if her sister was in town yet. Alice and her husband, Arthur, farmed on the opposite side of town, but Sally and Alice coordinated their days to drop off eggs and butter in town. If Alice had heard about the newcomers, she was probably already at the town pump.

Slipping her empty egg basket onto her arm, Sally joined a few others already headed in that direction. Mr. Granger, the baker, tipped his hat her way as he walked along without a word.

The pump was on the east side, near a grove of trees that beckoned travelers to take respite on their way through the wide, open prairie. The oak and beech trees were just beginning to bud, and today's warm sunshine seemed to hurry the process.

Two unfamiliar wagons rested in the shadow of the Finchville Arms, the only hotel in town. Finchville bustled just two seasons a year, planting and harvest. But it appeared anyone in town today, with the exception of Mrs. Gibbons, was at the pump now.

Her gaze fell on the newcomers themselves and her heart unexpectedly fluttered. Perhaps they weren't quite as large as Goliath, but each one tall, broad shouldered, sturdy and hard as the strongest oak. Four. . .five if she counted the patriarch in this family, judging by the thatch of thick gray hair above a still handsome but leathery face.

For a moment she wondered if this was some sort of ploy to get the townsfolk together and rob them all at once. Who would stop them? Sheriff Tilney wasn't the only one absent—she didn't see Willis or his father, the mayor, either. Had some other member of their so-called family diverted the town's only officials so they could be about their crime?

Telling herself she should have waited for Alice at the store, she started to turn back when one of the men stepped out from his pack.

"People! People!" rang his voice as he jumped on the iron bench near the pump. He waved onlookers closer. "Thank you for the warm welcome to your fair town!"

He was definitely not like the pictures she'd seen of the cruel warrior Goliath, always portrayed with a fierce scowl before meeting his unlikely death. If anything, this man was a matured David—someone who'd inspired more than one heroic story.

"Permit me to introduce myself and my family," he said as he crossed his chest with one palm and gave a quick bow. "I am Lukas Daughton and these"—now sweeping that strong palm to the men behind him—"are my brothers." Each one saluted as Lukas called a name: "Bran. Fergus. Nolan. Owny. And finally"—he leaned down to hold up one of the older man's hands—"may I present the best of us all, our father, Nathaniel Daughton, the finest engineer west of Baltimore."

He turned his attention back to the crowd, perhaps counting how many were present. When his gaze roamed he stopped at Sally before going on, but looked at her again—only to let his glance linger with a smile.

She looked away, hiding her face with the brim of her bonnet for fear he would see evidence of the blush his notice had ignited.

"Now why, you might be thinking," he went on, "does this family of burly men want to steal a few minutes of your day? Let me tell you we've heard of this little hamlet, with its sparkling creek and fertile farmland, and the forests to block the harshest weather the prairie offers. So we came out here to see for ourselves if this might be the place for us to do what we do best: build a grist mill that will serve not only your farms but those from this entire county."

Whispers erupted here and there, but Sally couldn't tell if her neighbors were interested or skeptical. While there were a number of small mills connected to towns between Chicago and Iowa, there weren't many and all were a considerable distance away. How her father would delight in being able to grind corn meal or flour right here in town!

And yet…she reined in her interest. That would certainly change things around here. "What's this all about?"

The call came from a familiar voice not far behind Sally. Mayor Silas Pollit, Willis's father, possessed a voice that fairly whistled, like a bullet before hitting its mark. Although he'd already been mayor when Sally and her family moved to Finchville three years ago, she'd always wondered if his voice was one of the reasons he'd been elected. No one could ignore such a grating, if commanding, sound.

"Ah!" The newcomer's voice carried, it had to be said, much sweeter on the ear. "I can tell by the cut of your coat you're a man of some renown." Yes, Lukas Daughton's voice was definitely easier to enjoy. Loud enough to be heard, yet smooth and easy as it slipped inside and coated the inner workings of her ear with pleasing tones. She wondered how he would sound in church, singing a hymn. If he went to church at all.

Willis Pollit had arrived with his father and took a step closer to Sally, greeting her with a silent, familiar smile. He touched her elbow, too, and she crossed her arms to let her basket dangle between them. Why had she never noticed how possessive Willis's touch must appear?

The surprising question filling Sally's mind was why such a motion from Willis should suddenly feel more annoying than it had only yesterday?

Chapter 2

Lukas Daughton believed a face was made for smiling, because it took so much more effort to frown. Usually sooner than later, most people proved him right. Smiling was contagious.

It didn't take long to guess the newcomer, the mayor, someone had called him, looked like he didn't find much to smile about. The comfortable creases in his forehead gave him away.

Undeterred, Lukas included the crowd in their conversation as he made his way closer to the man he no doubt had to convince, if he truly was the mayor.

"I commend you, sir, for guarding the best interests of these fine town folk." Lukas glanced around, starting in the direction of the young woman he'd spotted earlier.

Edging closer to the mayor had brought him closer to her. She was even prettier than he thought, with her creamy skin and wide blue eyes. How many shades of blue had God created? The shade in her eyes was surely the prettiest. And her skin looked softer than those kidskin gloves his father gave Lukas's mother on her last Christmas this side of Heaven.

Lukas started his familiar speech, knowing it so well he could let his eyes return often to the girl without losing his place. "My father was born in Ireland, the son of a miller. From his youngest days, he saw the workings of a mill, from the gears under the millstone to the buckets on the water wheel. Before long his father heard of another miller who wanted to build a new grist wheel in the next county, and so he sent his oldest son—my father—at just fourteen years old, to help with the construction and be an apprentice. That began my father's education of how the best mills work. Something that has benefited others already and will do the same for you. If you let us."

With a wave to remind everyone of his brothers, he added, "Together we have built four mills under our father's direction. Before that, my father worked on or repaired more than a half-dozen mills in Ireland. Here in America our four mills serve farming communities that are now centers of commerce and success."

"And how is it you aim to build such a thing?" the mayor asked, looking him over with an eye that didn't miss their humble clothing. "Newcomers around here bring their own investments, and I imagine this will be quite costly. How do you propose to fund such an ambitious endeavor if you don't intend to earn a living from it after it's built?"

Lukas patted the man's ample shoulder with just enough assurance and confidence to avoid any hint of condescension. "We supply the labor, as well as the most important element of all: the know-how. The rest—and by that I mean the cost of material—we humbly submit would be shared by the town that will reap the benefits."

"Ridiculous," the mayor grumbled, shaking his head so that his double chin wobbled. "Do you expect us to entrust our resources or hard-earned money to strangers?"

"We're happy to earn that trust." Lukas looped his thumbs through his suspenders, all the while keeping the girl within the periphery of his vision. He pulled out the newspaper clippings he carried in his pocket, and handed them to the mayor. Several stories recounted the names and successes associated with mills they'd left behind, complete with the Daughton name as builders.

"What makes you think we believe you didn't have these articles printed yourself, just to fool unsuspecting towns like ours?"

"We can show you letters of recommendation from our past customers. But you might think we wrote them ourselves." He winked at the mayor. "The articles name the towns pleased with our work, all four, and you can send for verification. In the meantime"—he smiled again in the general vicinity of the girl rather than straight at her, because he sensed shyness in her refusal to meet his gaze— "we can get to work on first things first. The friendship."

A young man standing between him and the girl took another step closer to Lukas, fairly putting her behind him. Lukas had noticed how close he'd chosen to stand beside her, but Lukas wasn't yet ready to believe the man's claim on her. He was likely related to the town official, unless the similarity in the curve of their frowning brows was coincidence. Why would such a pretty girl want to be part of a family so unaccustomed to something as easy as smiling?

"What's to make us believe the person you recommend we contact isn't some crony of yours, paid to say whatever you want us to hear? You might not even be the Daughton builders you claim to be, but frauds using their name and reputation."

"I can tell this is a town filled with clever people!" Lukas spoke with gusto. "I like that. Why not simply address it to the name of the town, in care of the sheriff, or the mayor, or some other official as you please? A postmaster? An innkeeper? A storekeeper? We couldn't possibly know where the letter would land, could we? But I guarantee everyone in each town we left will know our names and can tell you about the success with our mills. And you can ask for descriptions of us. Five such handsome men as ourselves are hard to forget," he added with another wink.

"Got to admit," said another from the crowd, "if we had our own mill the price of flour would go down. So would the price of bread at my bakery."

There were a few other interested comments, enough to make the mayor lift one hand while at the same time taking Lukas's arm with his other. Lukas tossed a glance to his father so he would follow as he allowed himself to be led away, expecting the interrogation at hand. He knew enough to cooperate if they wanted a chance at another job without a reference already among the town's residents.

Following the mayor, Lukas couldn't remember the last time he was so eager for a job to work out.

Chapter 3

Sally watched as the mayor led two of the newcomers away. Lukas Daughton certainly knew how to stir the interest of a farming community.

"I'm going to join my father."

Willis's voice startled Sally; she'd been watching the trio ahead of them. Of course Willis would be part of the meeting. What surprised her was her immediate interest in going along, too. She detained him with a touch to his arm. "It certainly sounds like a good opportunity for the town, doesn't it?"

"Don't be so easily taken in," he said quietly, glancing at the remaining Daughton brothers not far behind them, who were mingling with others.

Sally's heart thrummed in anticipation of the meeting.

Her father was out in the field, her mother at home with countless tasks, and her sister—where was Alice? If any one of them were here right now, they would want the *town* to make the best possible decision, not the mayor alone.

"You don't mind if I come along, do you?"

One of Willis's brows lifted, those brows that were thick and bold just like his father's. Happy or bored or fascinated, his mood was easy to read. Just now they said he was surprised but skeptical. "I can't think of a bigger waste of time."

"But. . . How often does such an opportunity come along? It's worth investigating, isn't it?"

He scowled. "These men likely offer nothing but flimflam. I'm sure my father will see the sheriff escorts them quickly out of town."

"But what if they really could build a mill? Wouldn't the farmers want to know about something like this?"

Willis didn't have the ample stomach his father carried, but he did have a certain softness about him. He was much better suited to the legal work he did for his father than for farming or other manual labor. Right now he stopped, crossing his arms in front of him the way his father did, and regarded her with interest.

"Do you mean to say you really do wish to attend a meeting in my father's office? Not just accompany me?"

"I want to tell my father about it, and if I sat in I'd have more information for him, wouldn't I?"

Willis's surprise gave way to amusement, the way he often looked at her when she raised a question. He'd told her more than once she should have been a schoolteacher, with all the questions she asked.

"If not me," she persisted, "perhaps you could bring Mr. Granger, or Mr. Gibbons, or one of the farmers. Someone who might benefit more directly from a mill—" She cut herself off, realizing she'd been about to infer his father might not be the most qualified person to make such a decision.

Before Willis could disagree—she could see one of his brows pulling downward, just as it always did when he was about to state the opposite opinion of anyone around him—Mr. Granger stepped between them.

"She's right, Willis," said the baker, revealing he hadn't a hint of compunction about having listened in on their conversation. "Your father may think he's protecting the community but he oughtn't make this decision alone. Why don't you lead the way?"

"I don't think—"

But Willis didn't finish, seeing Mr. Granger beckon Mr. Gibbons and two other farmers.

Emboldened that their interest reflected her own, Sally grinned and held out an elbow to Willis as if to escort him, if need be. He managed a smile then took her arm to loop it properly through his.

The mayor's office was on the second floor of the post office, since he was also the postmaster as the town had yet to afford a salaried mayor. Tall windows let in the summer breeze while offering a view of the prairie and farms surrounding the town. His office wasn't a large room, being a converted parlor designed for the private quarters of any postmaster. A large desk took up the center, and along one wall stood an impressive bookcase filled with volumes he'd brought from the East. English law books, he'd claimed them to be, as if possessing them added to his authority as mayor.

Just now he looked none too pleased to see his son and the entourage behind him. The telltale brows revealed annoyance, even when he let his glance fall momentarily on Sally. He was usually happy to see her, at least whenever she was with Willis.

"This is bound to be boring," Willis said in her ear. "Why don't you wait down in the post office and I'll see you home afterward?"

"That's all right," she said gently, as if grateful for his consideration. "I don't mind in the least."

He might have been right about the engineering features of a grist mill being boring, since that was how the discussion resumed once the mayor realized their visitors were there to stay. But as the older man spoke with quiet confidence how he would design such a structure, using the power of the river that ran alongside the town, Sally could see she wasn't the only one impressed by Mr. Daughton's proposal. Or at least by his calm poise and depth of knowledge so obvious in his answers to every question.

"We could be finished by harvest time of this year," he finished, "sooner if some of the young men in your town could volunteer to help out with the digging and lend an ox or two to remove some of the earth we'll be shifting. My boys are strong and hardworking, but can't work faster than they're able."

"You'll have to buy a spot on the river, and most of the parcels are already owned by various farmers," the mayor said. "That'll be expensive."

"We plan to build the mill right here in town, Mayor," said Lukas, in a voice so calmly assured perhaps he didn't expect the gasp that greeted his words.

"In town? But the river will power the mill, your father said it himself."

"And so we build a canal to capture the water for a mill pond." The immediate doubt spreading across the room didn't dampen the man's confidence. "We've already measured the distance from the springhead. All we need is the plot at the end of town, where our wagons now stand, and permission to dig between the spring and there."

Sally studied the faces around her, seeing the man's cool certainty impacted a few others as it did her. Perhaps they really could perform such a miracle as putting a mill right where it would most conveniently serve.

She was also more convinced than ever that her father needed to hear about this proposal. Their cornfield stood between the springhead and town.

She looked again at the man called Lukas, hoping to ask if he might talk directly to her father. He happened to be looking at her, and despite her inquiry she dropped her gaze. She wouldn't ask in front of everyone; it would be hard enough just to have his attention, let alone everyone else's. When she looked at him again she noticed he included Willis in his glance this time, with a question in his eyes. She looked at Willis, too, who hadn't seemed to notice the exchange.

Surely she imagined that. Why should he care who Willis was to her?

As the discussion shifted to cost and supplies, Sally tried to listen more intently. Her father would be interested in such details, but for some reason she had a hard time concentrating; she, who was always so good with numbers. She handled all of her father's accounts, with livestock and feed and seed, a job gratefully relinquished by her mother the moment Sally expressed her interest. Sally delighted in contributing to the family in a way they appreciated. Numbers never failed her. There was always a right and wrong answer to make sense of the books. Unlike life, which wasn't always so clear.

To her annoyance, her thoughts were muddled more than once. Surely the young Mr. Daughton couldn't have such a quick effect on her. Willis never flustered her this way.

When the meeting ended, Mayor Pollit agreed to let Mr. Daughton speak to the farmers and businessmen after church on Sunday, in the church itself, since it was large enough to accommodate everyone who might want to attend. Sally moved toward the door, but Willis touched her elbow again.

"I'd like to stay and talk to my father about this," he said. "If you'd like to stay, I can see you home afterward."

She shook her head. "No, Willis. I must find Alice. We were supposed to meet at Gibbons' store and I'm sure she must be looking for me."

He gave her a distracted half-smile. "All right." Reaching up, he stroked one of her cheeks. "I'll call on you later this afternoon?"

She nodded, catching sight of the two Daughtons who seemed to be waiting for her to exit the room before they did. Smiling at them politely, she led the way back outside.

Chapter 4

Watching that young man stroke this girl's cheek flared equal parts envy and desire for Lukas to gain the right to do the same thing. This wasn't likely the first time the man had touched her in such a familiar, friendly way. Perhaps he was her husband—in which case, Lukas's envy was entirely inappropriate.

There was only one thing to do, and that was to find out who this man was to her. Once they were outside the post office, he left his father two steps behind. To his delight the girl appeared to be waiting for them.

"Thank you for your interest in our proposal, miss," he said, using his friendliest smile. "And I'm sorry to be so bold by introducing myself, but since I don't know anyone in town yet, I guess I haven't much choice if I'm going to know your name. You already know mine."

"I wonder if you might speak to my father about your proposal?" she asked without answering his question. "He owns some of the land you might be interested—"

"There you are! Sally Hobson, I've been looking all over town for you."

Lukas couldn't help but welcome the exasperated woman interrupting them, if only for providing the information he'd been seeking. Sally Hobson. As sweet a name as she deserved.

The other woman was perhaps a half-dozen years older than the pretty girl at his side—she was a friend or sister, too young to be her mother, though she did wear motherly concern, especially when she glanced from Sally to him.

"This is Lukas Daughton," said Sally. She held her palm toward Lukas's father. "And Mr. Daughton. They've come to build a grist mill."

The woman's brows shot up with interest. "Have you? My husband will be glad to hear that, I'm sure."

Lukas decided to like this woman, even if he did sense she wasn't prepared to return the feeling. Yet. "Perhaps you might have your husband speak to the mayor. The project will need local support if we're to succeed." He turned back to Sally, where his gaze was so eager to go. "And we'll be happy to speak to your father. Perhaps we can schedule to meet back here this afternoon, or in the evening?"

"That could be arranged, I think," Sally said. "Where shall we look for you?"

"At the rooming house dining room. We've already learned the food is good."

Lukas held out his hand to shake the older girl's hand first, not because it was expected but because he could follow with the same gesture toward Sally. He'd already spied the woman's left hand, looking for a wedding band and finding none. Besides, if she were married, wouldn't she have included her husband in a discussion about the grist mill, like this other woman?

He shook her hand gently, finding her hand small, warm, and just as soft as he'd expected. But there was strength there, too, and one tiny blister at the base of her forefinger betraying that she worked at something other than just keeping her skin smooth. He held her hand too long, but he wanted her to notice, to return his gaze, and she did.

He tipped his hat again, watched his father do the same without having spoken a word, and they walked down the street in the opposite direction of the girls.

"You ought not break another heart, Lukas," said his father, low, but thankfully they were well out of earshot from Sally or anyone else.

He patted his father's strong shoulder as if he were the wiser of the two. "I won't, Pap."

Sally let Alice loop their arms together as they walked along the sidewalk. The sidewalk itself was new, built by Willis's school friend who came to town just last year. It was a vast improvement over the street's dirt, so eager to go muddy at the slightest hint of rain, but many of the nails had popped and some of the boards were uneven.

"So you think Arthur and Pa will be interested in supporting a grist mill right here in town? " Sally asked Alice.

"I do," Alice said, but she looked distracted, as if her thoughts were elsewhere. When she threw a glance over her shoulder, Sally guessed where her thoughts had lingered. "You know that man was flirting with you, don't you?"

Sally felt the heat of blood rush to her cheeks. "He barely said a word to me!"

"The way he held your hand like that, waiting for you to look at him." She sighed. "I can't say that I'd blame you if you were flattered. He's fine looking."

"Alice! He's a stranger!"

Her sister nodded, evidently back to her senses. "Exactly. So you better be careful around him until you know him. He's got his sights on you, though, there's no doubt about that."

"Even if he does, it wouldn't matter a bit to me." The words flowed off of her tongue with such assurance Sally impressed even herself.

"Oh?" Alice nudged Sally's side with her elbow. "I

didn't think Willis made you blind to anyone else. In fact, I thought you found him annoying."

"Of course I don't!" Now she, too, glanced around, just to be sure no one could hear such a private conversation. "I do find Mr. Daughton. . .well, appealing. But in his speech to the townspeople, he said they've built four grist mills already—"

"Really? How wonderful! They must have all the experience in the world."

"So that's what they do, Alice. They build a grist mill, then they move on to the next town and build another. I have no intention of getting caught up with someone for a summer romance only to be left behind when his job is finished."

Alice stopped their perambulation, smiling gently at Sally. "You've always been the sensible one in the family. And of course you're right." She led on again, giving Sally's forearm a squeeze with her free hand. "Maybe that shy streak in you is more protection than I imagined. It's given you the strength to control your heart better than I ever could. Once Arthur looked at me the way that man looked at you just now, I was entirely at his mercy. Yes, you have far more sense than I ever had!"

Sally walked along, telling herself her sister was right. Of course she was.

If Lukas Daughton would be staying, she knew already she must guard her thoughts. He was undoubtedly a flirt; he smiled at her in a way he hadn't toward either her mother or Alice. His smiles were slow, as if to extend how long he might politely look at her. And even though she reminded herself he likely chose a favorite girl to spend time with during the building of each grist mill, she couldn't help but recognize the growing warmth around her heart with each passing moment in his company.

She was only half surprised but entirely pleased when he detained her as the others walked from the dining room after their meal ended.

"I'd be pleased to escort you to church on Sunday morning, Miss Sally," he whispered.

Welcome as that sounded, she knew it was impossible. For the past month, Willis and his father shared the same pew with her family, right up front for all to see. It had been Willis's idea.

"I'm afraid I couldn't, Mr. Daughton. But I will certainly look forward to seeing you and your family there."

His smile went a little crooked, but despite her refusal, the pleasure on his face didn't disappear. "All right, no escort needed. Mind if I save a seat for you?"

Lukas Daughton was definitely easy to look at, and difficult to resist. Yet she knew any change in seating would require some kind of discussion between her and Willis. Besides, she ought not even consider sitting anywhere else. What would Willis think? She was not as eager to get married as Willis seemed to be, and as the entire town seemed to expect, but she knew she could grow fond of him if only because of his persistence. Most importantly, like Sally herself, Willis had no intention of leaving Finchville.

"I'm sorry, Mr. Daughton—"

"Lukas."

She couldn't help but grin, though she refused to be swept up so easily in his flirtation. "I'm sorry, but my family and I have been sitting with the Pollits for some time now, and I'm sure they would be disappointed in any change. And there isn't really room. . ."

"Ah," he said slowly. "The mayor and his son. So I should squash my wishes to shower you with my undivided attention?" His tone was light, even with the disappointment still lingering in that little furrow.

She glanced at her departing family. Only Alice seemed to have noticed that she hung back with Mr. Daughton, but she threw her a grin. Of everyone in town, only Alice supported Sally's unhurried pace toward the altar with Willis. Even her parents seemed convinced it was only a matter of time before she and Willis made an announcement.

"I thought your undivided attention would be devoted to the gristmill, Mr. Daughton."

"Lukas isn't such a hard name to say, is it? I'd love to hear you say it."

She couldn't stop the corner of her mouth from rising, but she refused to answer his wish. Instead, she squared her shoulders and listened to the sensible words forming on her own tongue.

"This is a small town, Mr. Daughton. One I will likely live in for the rest of my life. I can offer the same sort of friendship to you that the town will be prepared to offer to someone bringing the benefit of a gristmill. But that's all."

She turned, proud of herself for having issued such a speech without a hint of the shy nervousness that often plagued her when speaking to strangers. Somehow he already seemed less than a stranger, despite only having met him earlier that day.

She would have walked on, but he spoke again. "Let me ask one more question. Should I withhold my special attention toward you because your heart is already elsewhere, or because you don't trust how easily *you* might enjoy my special attention?"

Sally felt her eyes widen at his boldness, but no answer came to mind. Not a reproach for his diligence after she'd hinted her connection to the mayor's son, nor even a whisper to defend what so many people in town already believed about her and Willis.

Chapter 6

Change was coming, people said, and Sally didn't doubt it was true. For the first few days after the official vote was won, all anyone in Finchville talked about was erecting the mill. While no transformation could happen overnight, a gristmill to be built in a matter of months seemed to present swift change indeed.

She told herself she would grow with the town. She wanted her family and friends to prosper. She just hoped Finchville would stay the kind of town it was now, one where inhabitants either knew everyone firsthand or knew with whom they belonged. She wanted Finchville to stay a town that cared about its neighbors.

After two weeks of little change, life slipped back into what it used to be and Sally breathed easier. She rarely saw the Daughtons except at church, where Lukas Daughton chose to sit directly behind her. She learned he was polite, and had the kind of singing voice she'd suspected the first time she heard him speak. His presence, she had to admit, was a distraction she struggled to hide.

They began felling trees for the mill from wherever they were given permission, while the elder Mr. Daughton marked land that was to be dug. To her own consternation, she found herself eager for the day they would begin digging through her father's field. An eagerness she could only ascribe to seeing Lukas on a regular basis, a fact that tugged at her spirits each and every time she saw Willis.

Today, as she delivered her butter and eggs, she saw several townspeople gathered outside the store, and Willis in the center of the group. As Sally approached, Willis raised a hand in supplication to the two men he'd obviously been arguing with. "All I'm saying is that the location of the mill seems strange to me. Mills are powered by the flow of water. I still don't see how that will work with a building so far from the river's edge. It seems to me the Daughtons might be what my father and I feared: at best incompetent, at worst deceivers, here just to take advantage of our pocketbooks. They've admitted they haven't yet built a mill so far from the actual source of water."

"How are they profiting from this? We haven't paid

them a dime." It was well known Mr. Granger had allowed them to remove more trees from his land than anyone else.

"I just wanted to remind you that neither my father nor I have supported this, not from the beginning, and if it proves as foolhardy as we fear, we hope you know we'll still do all we can to right the matter when it falls apart."

Mr. Granger shook his head, but didn't say anything as he walked back in the direction of his bakery. The others soon dispersed, leaving Willis now smiling at Sally, as if nothing unpleasant had just taken place.

"Can I talk you into an early lunch?" he asked Sally. "I passed by The Arms' dining room today, and they're baking a meat pie I promise will be delicious."

"I'm sure it will be," she said, "but my father is expecting me out in the field, and I'll have just enough time to drop off my eggs and get back."

He shrugged, taking her elbow to direct her inside the store.

"I wonder, Willis," she said, "what the Daughtons must do to convince you that they know what they're doing?"

"I have my man out there watching them every day," Willis said. "This trench they're planning on digging isn't coming from the nearest section of the river behind town. They're digging a longer trench than necessary."

His man, Sally knew, was Cyrus, an older man who'd been with the Pollit family from childhood, Willis had once told her.

"Perhaps you could speak to Mr. Daughton if you have some concerns."

"Oh, we intend to, believe me. They may not officially report to my father, but you can be assured we'll keep a close eye on them every step of the way."

"Willis," she said, low, "I hope you're only doing this out of concern for the town."

Willis patted her hand. "Of course. Why else would I spend so much time thinking about this? Or spare Cyrus from his other duties?"

His smile, as always, was so sincere, his gaze so guileless, that Sally couldn't doubt him. Still, she wondered if the Daughtons might appreciate knowing they were being watched nearly every moment of the day.

Chapter 7

Lukas was the first to wake the morning he was to start digging the trench. They'd already dug a preliminary pit, butting up to what was to be the cellar of the mill—a cellar Fergus and Nolan were lining with limestone. The collection pond to hold water for running the mill's wheel would connect with the millrace he would dig, deep enough to tap into water flowing beneath the ice in the winter, allowing the mill to run year-round.

Today he would begin digging from the source of the spring, and be joined tomorrow by Bran, who would follow him and deepen the initial cut. The flow, according to Pap, was more important than digging the shorter distance from the portion of the river that ran closer to town. Their canal would divert some of the water exactly where they needed it to be, while leaving the rest of the river untouched.

He had to admit this was the portion of work he'd anticipated ever since learning who owned the land they needed to use nearest the fountainhead. Mr. Hobson had easily agreed, for a portion of the mill's future income, to let them take the back end of his cornfield for part of the canal. All day Lukas kept one eye on the horse-drawn slip scoops digging into the ground, and another eye on the Hobson house in the distance.

Though he'd gone out of his way to catch Sally Hobson's eye if he happened to see her in town or at church, Lukas had already learned quite a bit about her, in spite of spending so little time alone with her. He knew she blushed easily, chose her words carefully, prayed with her eyes closed, and looked at friends and family alike with open but quiet affection. He wanted her to look at him in such a way. . .but first he needed to figure out her relationship with the mayor's son. So far, he had reason to believe Sally wasn't exactly smitten with the young man, even if he was with her. Lukas wasn't in the habit of stealing other men's girls—unless, of course, they wanted to be stolen.

"Ho, there!" Lukas called to the horse hitched to the scoops that dug into the earth ahead of them. "Ho, Leonidis!"

There, coming from the house in the distance, across the new sprouts of corn, he spotted the very silhouette he'd hoped all morning to see. There was no mistaking that graceful, bonneted form—and she was coming his way.

Taking off his hat, swiping a forearm across his forehead to catch whatever sweat his hat left behind, he pulled off the leather shoulder straps he'd used to direct Leonidis, and stepped around the equipment. He wanted nothing between him and what he hoped was his own special visitor.

"Nice to see you, Miss Hobson," he said. "In fact, you're about the prettiest sight I could imagine."

Without meeting his gaze, she pulled something from the basket on her arm—a corked stone pitcher with a tin cup strung to its handle. She handed it to him and took out another item wrapped in a checked napkin. "I'm in the habit of bringing refreshment to my father when he works this field," she said. "He usually comes home looking like Adam before God's polish: all earthen as if he'd just been created."

Laughter burst from Lukas. "I guess I look like that already, and it's not even noon."

He welcomed her offering, seeing the napkin fall open to reveal a treat of bread, cheese, and a slice of cake. But most of all he was pleased with her company, and not only because she was so unexpected.

"My father enjoys two light lunches while he works,

one before noon and one mid-afternoon. I thought you might not mind an interruption."

"Pardon me for saying so, but you couldn't be farther from an interruption."

It was her turn to laugh now, and it made him marvel. It wasn't just her ready cheerfulness. It was how easily he enjoyed her company. Lukas had been on the receiving end of enough smiles and winks to be confident around women, but somehow this was different. He'd sensed intelligence in Sally from the first day she'd followed them to the meeting with the mayor. Lukas imagined he could talk to her about anything, and she would have something to say.

The sandwich and cake melted in his mouth, the cider—last year's batch, she confessed—sweetly chased down every crumb. But even as she waited while he enjoyed the treat, he saw something else on her brow as she scanned the clearing. She almost looked worried.

He might be a new student to reading her face, but he was certain he'd read her clearly. "Anything wrong, Miss Sally?"

"There *is* another reason for my visit. I wonder, Mr. Daughton—"

"Lukas," he said.

"—if you're aware of those who've been watching your progress? Not here, perhaps, but cutting trees, or digging at the mill site."

"Oh, sure," he said. "Boys, mostly. Not that I blame

them. When I was a kid we always prowled around looking for something of interest to see. Just wait until we raise the water wheel. That'll give them something to watch!"

"Local boys aren't the only ones watching," she said quietly, but not looking at him, as if she felt the town and everyone in it guilty of not believing in the quality of their work.

He finished the cider, handed the cup back for her to reattach to the jug. "I know. I've seen them."

"Then you should also know they're talking about calling another meeting. Evidently they're concerned about the placement of the mill, so far from the water."

"Let them. We know what we're doing."

She held his gaze steady for the first time, inadvertently giving him the opportunity to admire the blue flecks in her eyes. Various shades mixed together to create the color of the sky. *My, she's pretty.* He was surprised how comfortable he was in her presence. More than one girl had brought up the topic of marriage before he even knew a girl's temperament. Some girls didn't need much more encouragement than he'd already given Sally to start such thinking. But somehow he knew Sally Hobson wouldn't try nabbing anyone who didn't present the idea first, and whoever did would be lucky to win her.

"I believe you do know what you're doing," she whispered, and hurried away.

But her words were all he wanted to hear.

For the next four days, Sally delivered refreshment to Lukas—and to Bran, when he was there—as they worked behind her father's field. She refused to show her disappointment on the days his brother was there, or acknowledge the cause of her disappointment at not finding him alone. She brought larger meals when she saw more than one Daughton at the trench, but her real enjoyment was watching Lukas savor the meal, listening as he told her about the other mills they'd built, the towns they'd left in their wake. She'd always enjoyed listening more than talking, and Lukas didn't seem to mind.

On the fifth day when she headed back home after her visit with Lukas alone, she was surprised to see Willis's carriage waiting at the hitching post.

Entering through the back of the house, she paused to drop off the empty jug and basket, and left her bonnet on a chair beside the kitchen table.

"Is that you, dear?" her mother called from the parlor. "You have company."

She walked through the small dining room that separated the kitchen from the parlor, and greeted Willis with a smile that was in sharp contrast to the frown she saw immediately on his face.

"I came to speak to you, Sally."

"Then I'll leave the two of you to talk—"

But Willis was shaking his head before Sally's mother had finished. "You ought to stay, Mrs. Hobson. You'll want to know what I came to say."

"Goodness," her mother said, "that sounds serious. And here I thought you'd just stopped by because you haven't seen Sally since Sunday."

"That's right, I haven't. But my man Cyrus has seen you, Sally. Hasn't he?"

"Has he?"

"Yes. Quite a few times, in fact. Delivering refreshment to those Daughton men. Is that where you've been just now?"

"That's right," Sally admitted. She ought to be indignant that Willis sounded as if this was something to be ashamed of, but knew she couldn't be. If her visits had only been neighborly, perhaps she could have returned his attitude with a righteousness of her own.

Sally's mother was still smiling amiably, looping one arm through Sally's and the other with Willis. She led them to the sofa, as if a comfortable seat would forestall the possibility of disagreement. But no one sat. "Sally always delivers food to her father when he's out on our field. Seeing the Daugtons working so hard in the sun reminded us how much her father appreciates the refreshment."

"And it's been no trouble," Sally added.

Willis made an effort to lift his frowning brows,

but Sally saw it was too much for him to conceal the exasperation he no doubt felt. "Don't you see how it might look, dear? It's one thing to be naturally kind to your own father, but to deliver repast to a family you barely know—"

"The Daughtons have been here for weeks now, Willis. They've proven hardworking, and they all attend church and sing with the best of us. How can it be wrong to be neighborly?"

"But they're not neighbors and will never be," Willis insisted. "You must know they're only passing through."

"All the more reason to show them Christian kindness."

Willis's frown was in full view again, and he looked from Sally to her mother as if expecting her support. But she dropped her contact with him instead.

"I'm afraid I agree with Sally, Willis. I've helped put the refreshment together each and every day."

If he cared to extend the argument, he seemed to change his mind after neither one of them agreed with him. He smoothed his brow, with better results this time, and looked at Sally.

"I only brought it up because I thought you shouldn't go alone to carry out such a friendly duty. You are, after all, an unmarried woman, and the Daughtons are all men."

"I'm sure no one would think it odd to treat such hard workers with kindness in the openness of our very own field."

Willis didn't look placated, but he did manage a smile.

"Will you come out to the porch with me for a few minutes, Sally? Just so we could visit?"

She followed him dutifully out to the porch, where Willis sat a bit closer on the swing than she expected from someone so obviously concerned about what others thought. He smelled slightly of his midday meal, onions perhaps, mixed with peppermint that hadn't quite conquered the other odor.

"I think we ought to spend more time together than just sitting next to one another at church, don't you, Sally?"

"What do you have in mind?"

Willis looked at her, his eyes now warm, brows smooth. "I see no reason why we shouldn't announce a wedding date."

She let her gaze flutter away, knowing her usual shyness wasn't the culprit for her confusion over what to say now. "There is one good reason we haven't announced anything, Willis. We haven't really spent much time together. And besides that, you've never asked me to marry you."

His laughter sounded unexpectedly high, as if nervous. "I thought my intentions were understood."

"Did you?"

"Everyone expects us to marry, Sally." He inched a bit closer, slipping an arm around her shoulders. At least the peppermint seemed stronger now, with each word he spoke. "Haven't you noticed? Even your parents expect it."

"Is that a reason to marry?"

He laughed a peppermint laugh. "It certainly is. They're wise, and they support something that makes perfect sense."

"But why should it make more sense for you to marry me than for you to marry any other young lady in town?"

"You silly goose! You're egging me on, aren't you? Well, I'll succumb. I'll say it. I don't want any other girl in town. How could I? All my dreams are about you."

This was the first time Willis had spoken so directly of his feelings. As to seeing her in his dreams, she wondered what that had to do with love. Her own dreams rarely made sense, and had little to do with reality.

"Those are pretty words, Willis. But I'm not sure we know each other well enough to announce a wedding day. Besides, my parents depend upon me. I do all of the family accounting; did you know that? I'm not sure I'd have the time to run my own household and continue to help here as well."

"Surely your parents want you to have your own life, not to be shut away taking care of them."

"No, of course not. But until I figure out a way to do it all. . .living in town with you is a bit farther than I expected. I always pictured myself on a farm nearby, not all the way in town."

"Live out here in the middle of the cornfields?"

"Of course. The days go quickly running a farm. And it's lovely out here."

"You mean lonely, don't you?"

"You're proving my point, Willis. We hardly know one another. You would know I'm more comfortable with family and fewer visitors than socializing every day if I lived in town."

"It's only that you're not used to it yet. Once you're my wife and we're entertaining people who need my services as a lawyer, or those we'll know through my father, you'll soon learn to love all kinds of people passing through our door."

Sally pushed away immediate disappointment that he so quickly and easily dismissed her worries. Worse, the image of countless dinner parties left her dreading such a prospect.

Still, she must consider his words carefully. After all, Alice had been telling her for years that she needed to spread her wings, test herself in more social situations. Perhaps she really did have a gracious hostess inside of her. How would she know? She preferred spending time by herself, it was true, but that didn't mean she couldn't learn to enjoy the company of others. There were people at church she genuinely enjoyed and could easily imagine socializing with.

However, rather than a picture of Willis as the host and

she, his hostess, a sudden, unbidden image filled her mind. What would it be like to entertain with such a friendly counterpart as Lukas Daughton at her table?

Chapter 8

Spring planting ended as it always did, followed by plenty of chores, fretting over crops, neighbors exchanging goods rather than dollar bills. In addition to the eggs and butter that Sally sold or bartered through the year, she collected honey from the hives on their land to trade along with jams and berry pies she made with her mother. Their creations seldom sat long on the Gibbons' store shelves.

Although it would have been easy to do so, Sally didn't allow herself to deliver afternoon repasts to the Daughtons once their work returned to the mill site in town. As her mother reminded her, Willis was a dependable, popular citizen of their town. It wouldn't do any good to offend him. Besides, both she and her mother were so busy with berries and honey that the sunny days, as always, flew by.

But, as usual, when she visited town at an early time of day, she looked around for Lukas Daughton's familiar face. He seemed as privy to her butter and egg schedule as she was herself.

"Hold up there, Leonidis. Ho!"

Sally's heart skipped, recognizing not only the name of the horse but the voice bidding its halt. She turned, seeing Lukas pulling up in a wagon beside the store she'd just exited.

"Morning, Miss Sally," he called as he hopped from the rig. "It's a glorious day!" Tipping his hat, he stood close, towering over her.

"And what makes this day so good?"

"It's bound to be a good day when I see you."

Warmth flooded her cheeks in spite of herself. "Good morning, Mr. Daughton."

"It's Lukas," he said, and bent closer to whisper in her ear, "but you already know that, don't you? Now if only I can convince you to use that name instead of my father's, this day will be all the brighter."

She had no intention of admitting it was a struggle not to call him Lukas, since his name came so easily to mind. Lukas's charm was as consistent as his attention, but each passing day of progress on the mill brought his departure that much closer. That was enough to help her resist him—at least with her actions, even if her mind had already surrendered.

"I thought you should know your brother-in-law will be joining us next week, after he returns from his visit to Chicago with his most recent load of livestock. He's volunteered to work with us a few hours a day for the next two weeks."

"Yes, so my sister told me. My father hopes to help as well, now that you're raising the walls of the mill."

"We'll welcome whatever help we can get," Lukas said.

She began to turn away, thinking their conversation was at its logical end, but he detained her. "Your brother-in-law invited us to dinner tomorrow night. Will you be there, Sally?"

She knew about the dinner because Alice had slyly invited Sally, too. Sally saw right through her sister's intention to put her together with Lukas. Like it or not, Alice was a romantic. Sally being left with a broken heart at the end of the summer didn't seem to frighten her sister at all.

But the way Lukas had lowered his tone, the same invitation her sister had tried so casually to extend sounded downright intimate. Dropping the polite "Miss" before her name hadn't escaped her, either. That must be why she had such a difficult time tearing her gaze from his.

She knew what she must say, despite every silent objection demanding she say something else. "I–I'm afraid

I can't be there, Mr. Daughton."

"Why?"

She knew it was wiser to keep her thoughts to herself, especially those having to do with him. But she must make it clear she had no intention of welcoming his attention. "For the same reason I won't call you Lukas."

She tried to leave it at that, to walk on and let him draw his own conclusion, but he stepped in her path. It was a bold move, impolite even, but not unexpected.

His smile, though, erased every bit of his former surprise, as if whatever conclusion he *had* drawn bolstered his confidence instead of the other way around. "Most people," he said, his tone still far too captivating, "might think someone who is avoiding them doesn't like them. But do you know what I think?"

She lifted one brow, not daring to ask but not moving away, either.

"I think in some cases, avoidance means just the opposite. It's like someone who loves the taste of candy, but knows they'll eat too much and end up with a toothache. So they won't even look at candy. But it isn't because they don't like it."

"And you, Mr. Daughton, are like candy?"

His grin went lopsided as he nodded. "I just have to convince you I won't leave you with a toothache."

Perhaps not a toothache, but almost certainly a heartache. She bit back the words and walked around him.

"You realize the only way to prove me wrong is to show up?" he called after her. "Prove you can be indifferent to my company. I dare you to be there, Sally."

She didn't look back, just let her gaze dart away with the hope that no one else had heard him.

Chapter 9

O f course, she knew all along she would accept Lukas's dare. Not just to prove something to him, but to prove to herself she was every bit as sensible as she knew herself to be.

As she would have done for *any* dinner party, she wore her newest dress and took special care with her hair. She wished her parents were going, but the table in Alice's kitchen would barely seat the entire Daughton clan without adding two more places.

She arrived on foot at Alice's only a few minutes after six, and the door was already open to let in the breeze. Seeing the two Daughton wagons, she knew her arrival would draw everyone's attention and so rather than going in the front door she circled around to the kitchen entrance, where she found Alice.

"Oh! You've arrived just in time to stir the soup," Alice said, handing her a spoon.

Grateful that her sister was too occupied with dinner preparation to scold her for sneaking in, Sally set to work—knowing she couldn't avoid the rest of the evening for long.

Still, she put it off until dinner was served. She carried in a tray of bowls filled with soup, stealing a glance at the guests until her gaze stopped at Lukas. He hadn't noticed her yet; he was staring out the open door, as if looking for the latecomer. Her.

His gaze didn't find hers until Arthur invited everyone to sit at the table.

Proud of herself for having escaped any before-dinner awkwardness, she took her seat at last. She ignored Lukas's lingering gaze of appreciation, saying nothing as he claimed the seat next to hers. She thanked him politely when he played the servant and filled her glass from the pitcher of lemonade. And when their fingers grazed after they both reached for the bread, she pulled away as if burned, because that was how his touch felt. Like a lightning bolt that tingled throughout her body.

No one who knew her would think her quietness odd. Only she knew it wasn't just her shyness holding her tongue tonight. It was the sinking realization that if Lukas Daughton ever wanted to kiss her, she would be powerless to stop him.

And that was hardly what a woman, who might yet one day become engaged to another man, should be thinking.

At the evening's end Sally was both relieved and disappointed. Relieved she'd done nothing to encourage Lukas's attention—surely she'd won the dare—but disappointed because, inside, she knew she'd lost. Thoroughly and completely.

Eager to return home, to be alone to conquer her thoughts of him, she was the first to the door after helping Alice to clean up.

"You'll allow me to see you home, won't you?"

Sally shot a panicked gaze to Alice, avoiding Lukas's, who had stolen up behind her to ask the question.

"That's a fine idea," said Alice, much to Sally's dismay.

"But. . ." Sally's heart thrummed. "The stars offer plenty of light, and the road is wide between here and home. I'm sure I'll be fine on my own—"

"I wouldn't let you go off alone. It'll be dark soon," said Arthur, stepping toward the door as well. "Your father would have my hide."

Alice handed her the flour sack she'd filled with leftover cake, an offering to their father for having to miss the meal. The smile on her face was decidedly knowing. "Don't forget to give this to Pa."

"I'll carry it," Lukas offered. For the second time that

evening, his touch grazed Sally's and the same fire ignited, reminding her just how eager she was to be alone with him.

How was she to avoid this man when everyone else wanted just the opposite?

The rest of the Daughtons crowded into one wagon while Lukas helped Sally into the other. His father went ahead, and without a word, Lukas directed his horses to follow at a leisurely pace.

If she were less suspicious she might not have noticed the widening distance between the wagons. It was as if Lukas wanted no one overhearing them in the still night air.

"So?"

The single word might have confused someone else, but she knew instantly what he meant. She kept silent, pretending not to know what she fully understood the topic to be.

"If you can't deny it, I'll assume this evening proved you aren't indifferent to me."

"Mr. Daughton—"

"Are you going to call me that forever? Right up to the altar?"

She laughed at his words. Marriage was such a ridiculously unexpected idea, especially coming from him. "The altar, indeed."

He scratched his ear, laughing along with her. "I admit those words came as a surprise to me, too. But I've got to say"—he slid her a smile—"it's easy to see why they slipped out. It's nice having the prettiest girl in town believe in us."

She stared ahead. "I'm sure you've easily convinced a number of girls that you know what you're doing. And will no doubt do the same in the next town you visit."

His grip tightened on the reins; she saw the tension ripple across his knuckles. "This mill is going to be the best we've ever built. I've been thinking about staying to see it work."

"For how long?" Sally asked, heart thudding anew.

She followed his gaze to the nearby undulating land, the row of trees in the distance, and the setting sun still shimmering at the edge of the flat horizon beyond. The fertile ground would produce an unending source of grain to keep any mill working far into the future.

Though he didn't answer her question, he turned his gaze on her. "Sally, I've been patiently watching you in Willis's company since I came to town. Do you know what I see?"

She dared not speak, or even spare him a glance.

He went on anyway. "You look at him the same way you look at any other nice enough fella. You're comfortable around him, and if that's enough for you, maybe you'll be happy. But you don't look at me that way, and I'd like you to admit—to yourself if not to me—there could be more in life than just being comfortable."

A rush of warmth spread through Sally, this time without a single touch. She told herself she should be mortified, to be read so easily by a man she had no intention of encouraging. But even though she knew he was right, she still couldn't look at him for fear of what he would see in her eyes.

"Being comfortable is better than being heartbroken," she whispered. "So if you would please take me the rest of the way home, Mr. Daughton, I would appreciate it."

Chapter 10

Lukas had a good view of the horizon from a beam on the second floor of the mill. Already the landscape of Finchville had been redrawn, now that the second story was nearly complete. Though he scanned the view of town and beyond, Sally was nowhere in sight. He could use some of her sweetened, cool tea.

The thought of her made him smile, despite his growing fatigue. He'd enjoyed working with her father and brother-in-law whenever they could help out, but they weren't there today, with other farm chores demanding their time. Not that their presence guaranteed she would visit.

His hammer rejoined the chorus of his brothers, all perched on corners of the second story. For the past month he'd been hoping she would visit, but so far she'd stayed away. His hopes of seeing her today were about as parched as his tongue just now.

"Bran! Lukas!"

Owny had left them earlier for the shed they'd built on the other side of the millpond, where he was finishing his work on the millstones they would soon place inside the mill.

"Come quick!"

Lukas beat his brothers to the ground, alarmed at his brother's tone. Owny could jest with anyone, but never with a hue and cry.

Inside the shed, Lukas saw remnants of the millstone Owny had been grooving. Mined from local granite, it would have been hard to break, but it now lay in pieces in the center of the wooden floor. Their own sledgehammer was left nearby.

Horror filled Lukas at such a deliberate act, but no sooner had the realization hit him than his father, the last to arrive and closest to the shed door, turned on his heel. Lukas raced past, beating him to the small patch of bushes and weeds, an inconspicuous spot they'd chosen not long after receiving the town's approval to build the mill.

"They're all right," he called to his father, who had lagged behind Lukas and all three of his brothers. They'd placed the French millstone—the best stone to grind the finest flour—in the copse just to be out of the way, freeing their wagon of the ballast their horses had dragged all the way from Baltimore. These two stones were the last of the five pairs they'd purchased, having used the others in former mills they'd built between Finchville and Baltimore.

His father took a look for himself, and with a pat to Lukas's shoulder, directed them away from the spot.

"Who do you suppose did such a thing?" Owny asked.

Lukas was so eager to cast the name Willis Pollit that he barely caught himself in time. Who else in town didn't want their mill to succeed? It was no secret his father had hinted he could have hired someone from Chicago for the job, but it was Willis himself who most wanted the Daughtons to leave. Or at least Lukas. That much was obvious whenever Lukas smiled Sally's way—something Lukas had no intention of stopping.

"I'll go see the sheriff," Lukas said. "Owny, you'll need to scout another piece of granite. We promised a working mill before the first snow, and a working mill it'll be."

"What do you think of the idea, Mrs. Gibbons?"

The older woman's smile bounced between Sally and her sister. "Like it or not, that mill is here to stay. I say your celebration is the finest idea I've heard all summer."

Alice, who had met Sally at the store, fairly squealed with delight. Having the store keeper spread the word about Sally's idea for their "First-Fruits Festival" was a vital part of their plan. "And we'll have music, too! Think of all the harvest songs we know!"

As they chatted on about a celebration to honor the mill's opening, Sally's enthusiasm suddenly seemed more than just that. She felt hopeful, too. Enough people had doubted the placement of the mill that this celebration would go a long way to bringing the entire town together again.

Willis never hid his doubts about the mill. When he realized they could collect enough water to run the mill exactly where they'd placed it, he claimed the redistributed water would flood the town. But even Sally could see the center of the town stood on higher ground, and with the newly dug millpond and penstock directing the water toward the mill's giant wheel, it would take a great deal of water indeed to threaten even the deepest cellar on main street.

Her confidence in the mill seemed to deepen Willis's resentment, making his sullenness harder to bear his company. She refused to dwell on comparisons to Lukas, but somehow her heart did anyway.

However, believing in the permanence of the mill didn't mean she should trust the permanence of the Daughtons. Lukas may have hinted he would stay after the mill opened, but he'd never said for how long.

Alice looped her arm with Sally's, each with her own thoughts about the festival as they left the store. But shouting in the vicinity of the Sheriff's office caught Sally's attention the minute they stepped outside. Sheriff Tilney stood in heated discussion with none other than Lukas Daughton.

"I just don't know what you expect me to do about it, that's all," the sheriff was saying.

"You can ask around, starting with anyone you know who doesn't want the mill."

While the sheriff claimed he'd do all he could about whatever concerned Lukas, Sally caught Lukas's eye. He left the sheriff without another word and came to her.

"What happened?" she asked.

"Someone took a sledgehammer to one of the grinding stones," he said.

Sally's gasp matched her sister's.

"It didn't do more than send a message that somebody wants trouble," Lukas said. "We can make a replacement."

"But what a horrid message," Sally said softly. "Who among us could have done such a thing?"

Lukas's eyes narrowed nearly imperceptibly. But the quick gesture was enough to reveal his suspicions. Who didn't want the mill to succeed? Surely *Willis* wouldn't have done such a thing!

She stiffened, automatically defending the unspoken name—while at the same time determining to speak to Willis the first chance that presented itself.

Chapter 11

As usual on Sunday morning, Willis escorted Sally home from church. All morning she barely kept her mind on anything but talking to him—except she had no idea what to say.

It didn't help that Lukas sat nearby during the service. His silence dared her to confront Willis about the grinding stone, but his obvious suspicion made the impending conversation that much more serious.

At her father's wagon, Sally held back. "Willis," she said, "it's cooler today. Would you mind walking rather than riding?"

He looked delighted at the idea of walking back to her family home alone with her, which would take some time indeed, and her parents went off without another word.

"I certainly enjoy our Sundays," Willis said. "And you know why, don't you, Sally?"

"Willis," she began slowly. Many thoughts collided in her mind, no longer only about the grindstone, but other thoughts she'd been unable to conquer ever since Lukas had brought it up. Lukas was right; she was far too comfortable around Willis. She'd told herself that couldn't possibly be a bad thing, except she couldn't remember her heart ever fluttering at the sight of him, even when she'd first met him. She couldn't remember wishing for just the right words around him, fretting over her appearance, wondering if he thought of her as easily as she thought of him. Because the truth was she rarely thought of Willis unless she knew she would be seeing him. If she were as honest with herself as Lukas had dared her to be, she would admit even if she did feel occasional affection for Willis, it wasn't enough to consider marrying him. It wasn't fair not to tell him the truth.

"Yes, Sally?"

Forcing calm to her jarring thoughts, she stole a glance at him. "I thought you should know I can't consider marrying you." The words had nothing to do with what she'd planned to say, but she couldn't call them back and felt only the utmost relief that they were out.

"What?"

His shock nearly matched her own, but having a

suspicion that Willis might have crushed that stone was enough to convince her of what she'd just said. It didn't matter if she accused him or not; it wouldn't change anything, and she doubted he would simply admit it even if he had done such a thing. Right now, all she knew was that she wanted more to marriage than what she felt for Willis. That was true whether or not Lukas Daughton left town.

"I'm sorry, Willis," she said softly.

The initial hurt on his face turned to anger when a brow curved inward. "I was good enough for you before those mill builders came to town. That Lukas, anyway."

"No, Willis. I was wrong to encourage you, when I knew from the start I wasn't ready."

Now one of those brows lifted. "If I'm hurrying you, I can wait longer. I've already waited—"

She shook her head again. "My idea of marriage is. . .different from what I think yours might be."

"Why? Marriage is marriage. Faithful to each other, raising children together. How could your idea of marriage be different from that?"

"I just don't love you the way a girl should," she said at last, and the hurt in his eyes reappeared. "I didn't want to say that, Willis. But I don't know how else to explain how I feel."

He sucked in a breath as if she'd robbed him of air. "Well," he said slowly, stopping altogether. He looked at her, away, then back again. "I suppose you can see yourself home."

An overwhelming rush of guilt swept Sally. Perhaps she'd been too hasty; perhaps once Lukas was gone she truly would regret this decision. But those fleeting doubts weren't enough to stop the sensible words already forming on her lips. "Isn't it better to know I would be so hard to make happy, Willis? Now, rather than later? You would be unhappy, too, then, and it would be my fault."

He nodded, not looking at her, then walked back toward the main street where he lived.

Chapter 12

Rainclouds threatened to dampen the festival, so Mr. Daughton invited the women providing the food to set up refreshments in the wide, open second floor of the brand new mill.

Sally walked up the stairs, the scent of fresh wood and varnish mingling with the chicken and pies she carried on a large tray. As usual, she kept her eye out for Lukas, who had been especially polite but surprisingly distant since Willis no longer sat beside her and her family at church. But even if he had swooped in on her, she would have refused his company. She might have failed to keep her heart in check, but she would not encourage her growing love for him by spending more time with him before he left town. She spent enough time with him in her imagination.

Especially since it was no secret that Mr. Daughton was training Mr. and Mrs. Gibbons' oldest son, Charley, to work the mill after they left. That had been enough to seal Sally's resolve against Lukas, even though his face haunted nearly all of her thoughts.

Sally stepped into the large, open upper room, where planks and boards had been set upon trestles to hold all of the food for the party. Wind howled through an open window, rippling the cloths draped over the makeshift tables. Before she could drop off her goods to shut the window, someone beat her to it.

Suddenly the large and empty room was far more intimate. Lukas turned from the window, a welcoming smile on his handsome face.

"When I learned you would be working up here with the food," he said as he walked steadily toward her, "I volunteered to help. I even promise not to taste the goods until you give permission."

She laughed but knew she sounded nervous. And why shouldn't she be? She ought to run right out of this room, demand Alice take over. That's what Sensible Sally would do.

Instead, she stood perfectly still until he stopped, a hands width away.

"I want to talk to you, Sally," he whispered.

But before either could say another word, voices

clamored up the stairs along with clomping feet and laughter.

"Before the day is out," he added, and went to greet Mrs. Gibbons to help her with a basket of food.

Two hours later, the town gathered for the opening of the sluice. Water flowing from the spring some half mile away now collected on one side of the mill, to be released along the shaft running toward the huge wooden and iron wheel which turned the stones inside the mill. That same water spilled into the millpond on the other side of the wheel, where Sally now stood in anticipation of the mill's official opening.

She heard whispers from every direction, in one form or another: *the mill is a marvel of engineering*. Her heart swelled with pride—for the town, for those who, like her, never doubted it would work, for those like Arthur and her father who had worked on it alongside of the Daughtons. For Mr. Daughton who designed it. And for Lukas, because it had been his invitation that convinced others to let them build the mill right here in Finchville.

She knew he was destined to leave soon; she didn't expect anything else. But she would always have the mill, a shining spot of community and success, to remember the handsome young man who had captured her heart. Even if she never told him he'd done so.

No doubt the reason he wanted to talk to her today was to tell her good-bye.

With a wave to the crowd surrounding the mill, Lukas stood on the platform above the millrace, where the turn of a wheel would release the water and start the mill. Just as he did so, Sally heard another voice closer to where she stood.

"Lukas! Owny!"

Mr. Daughton shouted from the mill's cellar window, but the desperate call was drowned by the suddenly rushing water and turning wheel.

"Stop the water!"

Sally knew neither Lukas nor Owny had heard their father. But Lukas looked her way, and she frantically waved her arms, pantomiming to spin the wheel to shut off the source of water. Either he understood her motion or had heard at least the tone if not his father's words. Something was amiss below the wheel. Hurriedly he closed off the portal and Lukas and Owny ran to the cellar door and disappeared inside.

By the time she reached the same door, there was no room for her. Mr. Gibbons was already waving people away, preventing anyone else from squeezing inside the already crowded cellar.

The same whispers that only moments ago had touted the project a pioneering wonder were already abandoning their praise. *Too big a job. Some things just aren't meant to be built. I knew it would never work.*

Sally pressed forward again, determined to find out what had happened. She refused to believe anything had really gone wrong. Surely the mill wasn't a fancy shell of a failure!

Someone called for the sheriff, who was already nearby, and Sally stepped aside only long enough to follow him inside.

In the cellar's darkness, Sally could barely see. She searched for Lukas, but she was too short to see above the head and shoulders pressing into the cramped quarters. She couldn't even hear what they said to Sheriff Tilney, but before long the whispers started again. Intentional damage. Sabotage.

The outrage and suspicion in those whispers mirrored her own—but something else grew in Sally, and she stopped looking for Lukas. She slipped back toward the door.

Guilt filled her on waves of nausea.

Accusations made her heart sink. Willis had many reasons for the mill to fail. Damaged pride because no one listened to his distrust of the Daughtons. Avarice that he wasn't able to hire someone of his own choosing for the job, perhaps share in the wealth that was sure to come with such a town-altering improvement. And jealousy that it was Lukas who had changed Sally's mind about possibly marrying him.

It might have been Willis's actions, but the damage

was Sally's fault. She could have stopped him, if only she'd confronted him weeks ago about the millstone. Surely he wouldn't have been bold enough to ruin today if she had accused him when she had the chance.

The sheriff ordered people out, and for a moment it felt as if she were in the millrace itself, being carried outside on a current—not with water but with people.

She searched for Willis, someone she hadn't seen all day. She'd thought nothing of his absence until now.

Marching up the path toward Main Street, Sally quickly reached the post office building, where Willis lived with his father. But she barely had a chance to knock before the door swung open. There stood Willis, just straightening a crooked tie.

"Well!" he greeted her. "This is a surprise. I didn't think you'd want me as an escort when today will be the crowning glory for the Daughtons. Or have they left already, now that the project is finished?"

Folding her arms, she glared at him. "How dare you! How could you do such a thing?"

"What?" His brows rose indignantly but faltered ever so slightly—whether in anger or guilt, she couldn't tell.

"Someone tampered with the mill. Just as someone broke one of the grindstones a few weeks ago. Who else but you have hated the idea of this mill from the start?"

He raised both palms, but before he could speak something caught his eye from over her shoulder. She turned, seeing the entire town, led by not only the sheriff but by the Daughtons, coming straight toward them.

Sally caught Lukas's eye, who looked at her curiously. Perhaps he, too, believed if it weren't for her no damage would have been done, if only she had voiced her suspicions. Looking away, she stepped aside; no longer bold enough to make her accusations with the entire town ready to cast their own.

"You have anything to do with tampering with the mill, Willis?"

Willis's eyes rounded at the sheriff's question. Fear crept into his eyes as first one, then another man behind the sheriff demanded he confess.

"I don't know what any of you are talking about!" Willis protested. "I was nowhere near that mill. I'm a lawyer, you know. You'll need evidence if you want to make this kind of accusation."

"Somebody put this on a shaft above the gears," Mr. Daughton said, holding out a small metal object. "It was supposed to fall in and gum up the works. This yours?"

It was a simple shoehorn, something any number of people owned; even Sally's father had one. Willis looked at the object as if he didn't even know what it was. Even his telltale brows didn't give him away.

"Of course it isn't mine! I don't even own such a thing."

A commotion broke out at the side of the post office—shouts, pounding feet, a chase. Everyone turned to look, but when Sally looked again at Willis, his formerly rigid face filled with renewed fear at the sound of Cyrus's voice rising above the others. The servant cried out for all to hear. "I didn't mean it! I didn't even want to do it! But he—he made me do it!"

His finger pointed to none other than Willis Pollit.

Chapter 13

After a thorough inspection of the mill, Mr. Daughton learned several of the pins had been loosened along the millrace, inviting collapse. Rags had been stuffed in the hopper that fed grain onto the stones, and one of the mesh screens to separate grain from chaff was sliced.

The sheriff, however loyal he might have been to the Pollit family, had no choice but to take both Cyrus and Willis to the jail.

But repairs to the mill were completed in less than an hour, and once the mill proved it worked, any sourness toward Willis dissipated as the delayed celebration began.

Lukas searched once again for Sally, but he hadn't seen

her since the confrontation with Willis. Looming worry edged closer. Perhaps she thought Willis needed her, now that he hadn't a friend in town. Even his father, ashamed of the damage his son had arranged, or perhaps still eager to hold on to his job, stayed at the festival and openly derided what had been done.

It was already growing dark, and the sound of music carried over the gently spinning mill amid conversations and laughter. Lukas was more eager than ever to find Sally. This festival was her idea, and he'd planned from the moment he heard about it to say all he needed to say to her. Tonight. He was tired of waiting, of giving her time to make sure she didn't regret that she no longer allowed Willis Pollit to sit beside her at church.

If only he could find her.

Sally watched the festivities from the second floor window, in the room now emptied since the weather cleared and the leftover food had been taken outside. The earlier storm had passed through quickly, blessing the rest of the day with fresh air and now with starry skies. She stood at the very window Lukas had closed earlier, enjoying the sounds from below but without a sliver of desire to join the party she herself had suggested.

"Do you know I've been looking for you all evening?"

The deep voice should have startled her, but the sound

was far too welcome. She'd spotted him several times while he passed through the crowd below. Now and then he stopped to talk, to Alice and Arthur, to her parents. To his own father and brothers. He'd never lingered long, lending credence to the search he'd just confessed.

"I like watching people enjoying one another's company," she said, warning herself silently to keep the conversation light. No use saying anything silly just before he left.

He stopped at her side. "Only watching?"

The room was lit only by moonlight streaming in through the new glass. The quiet room and shadowy light added intimacy to the moment, making it more difficult than ever for Sally to tame her tongue and speak only politely. Her mind filled with the truth she couldn't reveal. She wished he would stay. She would never forget him. And the most secret truth of all: she'd fallen in love with him.

"I like people," she admitted. "But at a distance."

"Me, too."

She laughed. "You, who can talk in front of crowds, who charmed this entire town into letting you build the most ambitious business it's ever known?"

"Just because I can act like a salesman doesn't mean I like it." He leaned against the wall, no longer peering out the window with her. "In fact," his voice softened, slowed, "I think I'm better suited for steady work than essentially being a traveling salesman."

"Oh?" Her heart was beating so painfully it throbbed all the way up to her throat, so that single word nearly choked her.

"Can you hear the wheel still going, turning that grinding stone down there?"

She nodded, grateful for the return to lighter fare.

"There are two sets of stones for spinning, you know. One for coarse and one for fine. The finest flour will come from only one set of stones, and that's the set we brought with us. My father bought them in Baltimore—the only place in the country you can get French grinding stones. That was the last set we owned."

"So. . .I suppose your family will have to go back East again. For more stones."

He shifted to look out the window again, bending closer to her, and pointed toward his father at one of the tables. "He's a brilliant man, my father. He wanted to build the best mill possible, and this"—Lukas raised both palms to take in their surroundings—"is it."

"I'm glad he built it here, then."

Leaning so close to the window had brought his face only inches from hers. "This is the last mill he intends to build, Sally."

She wanted to read into that statement, but refused to jump to the best possible conclusion. "I suppose he's taught you and your brothers all you need to know to carry on, then."

He held her gaze, his lips curling into a smile. "Yes. My brothers could build more mills."

"And. . .you?"

His gaze slipped to her mouth then back to her eyes. "I'm staying right here to run this mill, Sally; with my father."

"But. . . But you hired Charley Gibbons!"

"Yes. So?"

"Isn't he going to run the mill?"

Lukas laughed. "Run the mill? All by himself? A man with one summer of training?"

"You're staying then?" The question seemed needless, but she wasn't convinced. "For a while, just until you're sure it's being run properly?"

"No." He drew out the word. "I'm going from mill builder to miller. I'm finished traveling every summer to a different town. I want a home."

"Do you?"

He stood only inches away, yet he took a tiny step closer. Close enough to feel his breath on her cheek. "Home, Sally. Here. With you."

Then he took her in his arms, kissed her gently, and she did exactly what she'd always done when she'd imagined this moment; she threw her arms around him and kissed him back.

Pulling away at last, she saw his smile illuminated so clearly in the moonlight. But then he put on a frown.

"Your kiss isn't quite convincing enough, Sally. There's only one way you can convince me that you want me to stay. Do you know how?"

She laughed, keeping her arms tight around his neck. "I want you to stay. Stay. . .*Lukas*."

He swept her up into a spin, kissing her again then whispering, "That's closer, my love. But I need to hear the words I see in your eyes."

She'd imagined saying the words so many times they drained away her shyness. "I love you, Lukas."

"Ah, Sally, that's what I've waited to hear. I love you, too."

Then, pressing his lips to hers, he spoke in spite of the kiss. "Will you marry me?"

She let her lips answer for her.

Maureen Lang writes stories inspired by a love of history and romance. An avid reader herself, she's figured out a way to write the stories she feels like reading. Maureen's inspirationals have earned various writing distinctions including the Inspirational Reader's Choice Contest, a HOLT Medallion, and the Selah Award, as well as being a finalist for the Rita, Christy, and Carol Awards. In addition to investigating various eras in history (such as Victorian England, the First World War, and America's Gilded Age), Maureen loves taking research trips to get a feel for the settings of her novels. She lives in the Chicago area with her family and has been blessed to be the primary caregiver to her adult disabled son.

The Wildflower Bride

Amy Lillard

Chapter 1

The Ozark Mountains
Calico Falls, Arkansas, June 1871

M addie?" Grace Sinclair poked her head through the door of the downstairs guestroom then stepped inside.

Her sister whirled around, cheeks flushed, eyes sparkling. She ran trembling hands down her pale blue wedding gown. The satin fell in beautiful folds, edged with a cream-colored lace that suited her sister so well. It might be all the rage for the bride to wear white these days, but no one ever accused Maddie Sinclair of being like everyone else. Her younger sister was her own person, through and through. "Is it time?"

Grace nodded.

"Is he out there?"

"I haven't looked, but I don't think Prissy would have sent me to get you if he was missing."

Maddie nodded and swallowed hard.

"You're shaking," Grace said, taking her sister's hands into her own. "And cold." It was a beautiful June morning yet Maddie's fingers were like ice.

"I'm nervous." Maddie warbled out a smile.

"Not about his love for you?"

She shook her head. There had been a time when Maddie had worried about Harlan Calhoun's love. Or rather, the honesty of that love. But Grace supposed that's what happened when a young woman plied the man she loved with cookies doctored up with a love potion. Suspected love potion, she corrected. It turned out that the herbs Maddie had traded her second-best dress to Old Lady Farley for were no more than ground nutmeg and vanilla bean, with a little cinnamon thrown in for good measure.

And that Harlan's love for her was real.

"Then what's wrong?"

Tears welled in Maddie's dark green eyes. "Nothing. Everything. I'm sad and happy and nervous and. . ." She shook her head.

"Sad because Mom isn't here with us?"

Maddie nodded.

Grace could only imagine how her sister felt. And it was a feeling that she herself would never get to experience.

She wasn't being pessimistic, just realistic. That was her, Pragmatic Grace Sinclair, destined to be an old maid. Though she preferred to think about it as giving her life to the Lord. Her destiny had been revealed long ago. She would stay in Calico Falls, never marry, and continue to help her father with his church.

She pushed those thoughts away and lifted her sister's chin. "Don't cry. It'll make your eyes all red. That's not how you want to spend your wedding day, is it?"

Maddie shook her head, her dark brown curls swaying with the motion. Even with tears in her eyes and her lips red from where she had bit them, Maddie was the prettiest bride Grace had ever seen.

"Then come on now." She passed Maddie a handkerchief. "Dry your eyes. Harlan's waiting. It's time to get married."

At the mention of her beloved's name, the sunshine broke free of the clouds, and Maddie's face lit up with a perfect smile. "Harlan," she repeated, her words a whisper of awe.

She wasn't jealous, Grace told herself. Envy was a sin. She was glad that Maddie had found the happiness that every woman deserves.

Then why can't you have it? That tiny voice inside her asked.

Because I'm fated to something different. A higher calling. At least, she liked to think of it that way.

Maddie took a deep breath and smoothed her skirts once again. "I'm ready." She smiled and held out her arm for Grace to take, and together the two of them made their way out to the back porch.

Birds chirped from above, the light wind rustled the leaves in the trees, and sunshine sparkled on everything it touched. God had spared no beauty on this day.

Across the yard a trellis had been set up, intertwined with colorful wildflowers and green ivy, the perfect backdrop for the joining of two lives.

And in front of that white-painted trellis stood their father. Pa blinked back tears. Grace understood. She had already shed a few of her own. But he managed to keep them at bay as he waited to marry his youngest daughter to the newest member of the community, Harlan Calhoun, attorney at law.

Harlan shifted from one foot to the other as Maddie and Grace approached. He looked nervous, happy, and little bit sick. And next to him stood—

Grace stumbled. Beside her, Maddie gasped and clutched her arm a bit tighter as if her grasp alone could keep Grace upright. She recovered quickly, managing to steady her steps, thankful she hadn't fallen flat on her face in front of half the town of Calico Falls. Later she would blame it on the uneven ground and the new shoes she had sent for, just for this occasion, but the truth of the matter was standing right in front of them. Suit-cut jacket and vest, pristine white shirt, wide black tie, and kilt.

The man was wearing a kilt. Somehow on him it was attractive, earthy and real, though she had never seen a man dressed like that before. Their laidback Arkansas town had everyone dropping the formalities that were often found in the big cities, like such formal dress at a morning wedding. Not that they were lax, but just a little less. . .ceremonial. If there were any Scottish residents in Calico Falls, she couldn't think of even one. And they surely didn't go around dressing like that.

To make matters even worse for her heart, he was the most handsome man she had ever seen. Dark, rusty hair the same color as her father's favorite horse, broad cheeks, thin nose, and eyes that even from this distance she could tell were as blue as the sky above them.

But she already knew his story. His name was Ian Mc-something and he lived back East. He was Harlan's best friend and had only come to Calico Falls for the wedding. He was staying less than a week and then heading back.

Why, oh why, Lord? Why was the only man since grade school who had set her heart to fluttering the one man she could never have?

Ian watched the bride approach. Well, that wasn't exactly

true. He was facing the direction from which she was coming. Yet it wasn't the love of his best friend who captured his attention but the woman at her side.

He had only just arrived in Calico Falls the night before and hadn't had a chance to meet all of Maddie's family. But he suspected that the blond-haired dream walking next to Maddie Sinclair was none other than her sister. Grace.

Grace. What a fitting name for such a lovely creature. *Ach*, she was the prettiest thing he had ever seen, or as his grandfather, Athol, would say, "A bonnie lass indeed."

During the actual ceremony, he found himself staring at her instead of paying attention to the service. He missed his prompt to give Harlan the ring and despite his friend's personal excitement on the day, Ian suspected that Harlan knew. He hadn't gotten to be the best attorney in these parts without being sharp enough to see what was straight in front of him.

"I now pronounce you man and wife."

Harlan tugged his bride a little closer and cupped her cheeks in his hands before placing a chaste kiss on her forehead. His hands shook with happiness and what Ian was sure was a bit of groom jitters, but he would have traded places with him for almost anything on God's beautiful earth. Well, if Grace Sinclair could trade places with her sister.

Ian tried not to visibly shake his head. What was

wrong with him? He was contemplating marriage and he hadn't even talked to the woman. Never mind that he was leaving in a couple of days. His original plan had been to stay the whole week, but summer rains had delayed his journey from the start, and just before he left, he was approached by the First Church of Albany, the largest and most prestigious church in Albany, New York. It was a progressive church, looking for young leaders to take them into the turn of the century. Well, so that wasn't for another thirty more years, and by then he would be anything but young, but the offer was too good to turn down. They wanted him back by Sunday's service to get started in his position as the assistant pastor there. That meant leaving Monday, Tuesday at the latest, to give him plenty of time for the journey and then to prepare for his sermon.

"Ian."

He startled as Harlan hissed his name. "Oh." It was time to leave. He looked around to find Grace staring at him, a small smile playing at her soft, pink lips. "Oh," he said again, realizing that he probably looked about as idiotic as any one man could.

Grace held out her arm and he took it, helping her back through the carpet of grass and around the side of the parsonage. The preacher's words floated over their heads, stating a noon meal would be served followed by the cutting of the wedding cake.

Ian didn't need to look behind him to know that the crowd who had just witnessed his best friend's wedding was headed their way. The murmur of the men's voices and the rustle of crinoline followed them and grew louder with each step.

"We're sitting at the family table inside," Maddie said, blushing with the words. It wasn't an embarrassed color, more of a delighted flush at the knowledge that she had joined her life with another.

Ian was happy for them, so very happy. He climbed the stairs with Grace at his side. She felt elegant on his arm, complete, as if a piece of himself long missing had finally found its way home again.

The inside of the house invited with warmth and style. The furniture wasn't what he'd expected, but then he clamped down on that thought. That made it seem as if he thought everyone in Arkansas was uncouth; that wasn't the case at all. He was just surprised at the fine things and treasures scattered throughout, and the beautifully crafted furniture that bespoke of an unexpected sophistication.

The dining room table had been set for the family. Three other tables had been placed in the parlor so everyone could be close. The promised wedding cake was set up on a table draped with a white cloth. Candles on beautiful silver holders winked at him, their flames seeming to know his secret.

Harlan had said that Maddie wanted everyone to eat outside and enjoy the beautiful day, but Prissy, the Sinclairs' feisty, cocoa-skinned housekeeper had set her foot down and said she wasn't toting all that food outside.

Reluctantly, Ian let go of Grace's arm and allowed her to move about, searching for her place at the table. With a groan, he realized that in all the time he had been walking right next to her, he hadn't said one word to her. He was worse than a school boy with his first crush. But the truth of the matter was he wanted to get her alone, talk to her all night and until the dawn, and find out everything he could about this woman he had fallen in love with. Yes, might as well admit it. He was in love with Grace Sinclair. He had never been one to believe in the nonsense of love at first sight, but his grandmother had always told him that God made someone for everyone, and one day he would meet his true love. He just never thought it would be today.

There was that word again. Love. But he loved Grace as surely as if he had known her his entire life. It was like destiny, or fate, or. . .God's plan for his life.

But he had no idea what God was thinking when He gave him this. *Trust in the Lord*, the Bible said. And he was trying.

He surely didn't want the first words out of his mouth to be a declaration of that love. She would think him mad and avoid him for the rest of the evening. Come to think of it, that might not be a bad plan. How was anything supposed to come of this love when he lived hundreds of miles away?

"Do you mind if I sit here?" He pointed to the chair directly in front of him, only then realizing that he had placed himself across from the bride, and Grace was heading for the seat next to his. Easton Sinclair had taken his spot at the head of the table, with Prissy sitting opposite him. If anyone else found it strange they didn't say as much, and Ian suspected that the housekeeper had more than a working relationship with the family.

He was secretly thrilled to be sitting so close to Grace.

Once everyone was settled, Prissy stood and made her way to the kitchen, directing the host of young girls who were serving them. When all the guests had a plate, she returned to her seat. Easton asked for everyone's attention and said a heartfelt blessing over their food.

Light conversation started up all around him, but he kept quiet. It was time he got himself in hand before he said something to embarrass them all.

He forked up a bite of his perfectly fried chicken. It was halfway to his mouth when Maddie spoke. "So Ian, Harlan tells me you're a preacher."

He lowered his fork and smiled at the bride. "That's right."

Up went the fork again.

"That must be fascinating," Maddie added.

Fork down. Ian nodded. "It can be." He raised his fork once again.

Before it touched his lips, Maddie said, "And you've just been accepted at your first church?"

Fork back down. He smiled at Maddie. "That's right. The First Church of Albany."

Something brushed against him under the table. He moved out of the way as best he could before trying for the bite of chicken once again.

"So. . ." Maddie started.

Whack!

What could have only been a swift kick sent pain racing up his leg. The bite of chicken he had managed to finally put in his mouth was sucked back and down his throat without the benefit of chewing. He sputtered and coughed, reaching for his water glass to wash down the ill-fated hunk of chicken.

"Don't just sit there, Grace, do something." Maddie jumped to her feet then sat back down as Grace sprang up.

She patted him between the shoulders, softly at first, then with increasing strength until he didn't know which hurt worse, his throat, his leg, or his back.

Her arm swung back again, but he caught her hand in his own before she could make contact another time. "I'm fine now. Thanks." His voice cracked at the end and his words were more of a croak than English, but Grace seemed to accept it and gently pulled her fingers from his grasp.

That in itself was a good thing. Her skin was soft, and she smelled so sweet he suspected if he spent any more time holding her hand he would assuredly embarrass them both.

Instead, he allowed her to move back to his side and return to her place at the table. Ian ducked his head over his meal and tried to concentrate on getting his food down. Chew, chew, chew, swallow. He could do this. Then after he ate he would figure out what he'd do with this crazy love he had for the woman at his side.

"About your church," Maddie started again.

"He doesn't want to talk about the church," Grace interrupted.

"Oh, I think he does." This from Maddie.

"He doesn't." Grace's tone turned stiff.

"Girls." Easton Sinclair didn't raise his voice at his daughters. Ian couldn't help but wonder if they did this sort of thing often. He was an only child, and the banter and teasing between siblings always fascinated him.

"Maybe we should talk about something else," Maddie said, her voice sweet and compliant.

Ian was ready for her to start gushing about the wedding; instead she turned her attention to him and said, "Doesn't Grace look beautiful today?"

He swallowed before answering even though he didn't have any food in his mouth. The moist chicken had somehow turned dry in the time since this conversation had started.

He glanced toward Grace, barely looking at her as he answered. "Very beautiful." In fact, she looked more beautiful than he had ever seen any woman look in his entire life. Ever. Wait, he had already said that. But she did look. . .beautiful.

"The two of you would make such a good couple," Maddie gushed. "Don't you think so Harlan, dear?"

His best friend shook his head then raised his napkin to his lips. Ian had seen that move too many times to count. It was Harlan's way of hiding his mirth and pretending that everything was fine. "I think it best that I bow out of the conversation."

"Oh no, my friend." It wasn't really the conversation he wanted to have, but Ian was stuck with it all the same. And if he had to participate then Harlan did, too. "What do you say? Would we make a good couple?"

Whack!

Again with the swift kick to the back of his calf, but this time he could tell that it was from Grace and had not been intended for anyone else.

He smiled at his friend and without looking away from him, reached under the table, and clasped Grace's hand in his own.

He wouldn't think about how easy it was for him to find her, as if he had some sort of previous knowledge of where she was. Nor was he going to think about the softness of her skin.

He gently squeezed her fingers. She squeezed back, in warning or affection, he wasn't sure. Maybe a little of both.

Harlan's eyes twinkled as he gave a pointed nod toward Ian and the spot where the table concealed their intertwined fingers. Ian hadn't realized it until that moment but he had leaned in a little to be closer to Grace. And she had done the same.

He straightened quickly and she followed suit, but it was too late. Everyone at the table had seen and they all were forming their own ideas about the matter.

"Oh I think the two of you would make a fine couple," Harlan said with a smile.

The bride and groom stood on the front porch, gazing out at the remaining guests. Maddie had changed into a traveling dress, this one darker blue, but just as beautiful as the one she wore to get married. Harlan looked as handsome as ever. Perhaps that's what happiness did to a person, made them more attractive than they had been before. If that was the case, then Grace had to be glowing with happiness. She was so very aware of every move Ian made the entire time they sat at the dinner table side by side. She had wanted to turn to him, whisper in his ear that maybe later they could go for a walk and talk about. . .things. But all she could see down a road like that was heartache. Maddie had already said that he was going back to New York soon. Despite Grace's immediate feelings for the man, nothing could come of it.

"All the single girls get on one side of the yard together. I'm going to throw my bouquet." It was a fairly new tradition that Maddie had heard about from a traveling salesman. Grace thought it had a certain charm, but seemed a little on the silly side all the same. Yet she went to stand good naturedly with all the other single women.

"One. . .two. . ." Maddie counted down. "Three!" She reared back and threw the bouquet toward Grace.

Instinctively Grace raised her hands and caught the bundle of flowers before they smacked her in the face. From her place on the porch, Maddie jumped up and down and squealed as if she had just received the best news of anyone in the world. "You're getting married next!"

Chapter 2

The next to get married. The words rang in Grace's ears as her sister and Harlan prepared to leave. That was the tale: if a single woman caught the wedding bouquet, then she would be the next to get married, but Grace knew better. She knew everyone in the town, and though the men all seemed nice enough, none of them were for her. None of them sent her heart fluttering like Ian McGruer. Bouquet or not, she would be an old maid. She wasn't happy about it, but that was simply the way it was.

Grace watched her sister go, her heart heavy. She couldn't remember a night without Maddie. They were more than merely siblings. Maddie was her best friend. Now she was off with her husband on a two-day honeymoon. Monday, they would be back, but nothing would ever be the same.

She felt his presence before he spoke. How could she be so in tune with someone that she could know he was there without even seeing him?

"Can we go for a walk?"

"No." She shook her head. That was the last thing she needed to be doing, walking and talking with Ian. Wanting more, for things to change.

"Please, I just want a chance to talk to you."

How could she tell him no? She nodded, and he offered her his arm.

Together they walked down the lane that led toward the field separating the main house from the adjacent land where Harlan was building a house for Maddie.

Colorful wildflowers washed the field in a variety of colors: red, purple, white, and yellow.

"I picked Maddie's flowers from here," Grace told him, needing to break the silence between them. It wasn't necessarily an uncomfortable silence, but she needed to say something to disrupt the intensity. Never before had she been with someone she had just met who she felt like she had known forever. Never before had words not been necessary in getting to know another.

"And you caught the bouquet. . ."

She shook her head. "Silly superstition. Besides, she wasn't supposed to be facing the crowd when she tossed it."

"You think that matters?"

"I think she threw it to me on purpose."

They walked in silence for a bit longer then Ian cleared his throat. "Can you feel it, too?"

"This. . ." she trailed off, unsure what name to give the unlikely miracle that was happening between them.

"I don't know what to call it but. . .I saw you at the wedding, and I just knew." He stopped and turned to face her, taking both of her hands into his.

"What did you know?" she whispered.

He gave a nervous chuckle. "That you were the one God made for me."

She closed her eyes and took a deep shuddering breath. "I know, but—"

He shushed her words, placing one finger over her lips. "You don't have to say anything. I know how impossible this is. And knowing that you feel the same. . ." He gave a bittersweet laugh. "Well, knowing that you feel like I do doesn't help at all. In fact, I think it's worse."

"What do we do about this?"

"I have no idea. I almost feel like God is playing some kind of trick on me."

"God doesn't play tricks on people."

"Really? Tell that to Job."

She gave a small nod. "So now we're back to what to do." She couldn't see any answer. There was none. He was leaving, she was staying, and that's all there was to it.

Maybe God was playing a trick on him. But if the joke was on him, it was on her as well.

"I don't think there's anything for us to do. I'm taking over my church this weekend. People in Albany are depending on me."

"I figured my life would be here, with my father. Helping him with his church."

"That's noble."

"I've just always thought that's what God has planned for me."

"Too bad He doesn't send a burning bush or angels these days. I could sure use a definite idea about what He wants."

She could only nod.

"I love you," he said. "I know that sounds mad, but it's true. And though there's nothing that can come of it, I just wanted you to know."

Grace squeezed his fingers and closed her eyes against the threatening tears. "I love you, too." And there wasn't one thing they could do about it.

Grace left Ian standing in that field of wildflowers and went back into the house. It seemed unnaturally quiet without Maddie underfoot. Or maybe it was the stab of jealousy that had her feeling so down. There. She admitted it. She was jealous of her sister. Jealous, jealous, jealous.

Long ago, Grace had settled herself to the fact that she would never marry. But was it Maddie's marriage or Ian McGruer's clear blue eyes that had her wishing things could be different?

"Gracie, is that you?" Her father called from the parlor.

"Yes, Pa." She started for the room, passing through the kitchen to check on the cleanup. Ever efficient, Prissy and the teen girls she had hired for the occasion had everything under control. Prissy waved away her offers of help before Grace could even voice them.

She flashed the woman a grateful smile then made her way to the parlor.

"Well, I guess that's it," Pa said as she came in and settled herself down on the settee. He had his pipe in one hand and yesterday's paper in the other. "I think everything turned out fine. You?"

Grace nodded. "The cake was a big hit." Last Christmas Harlan had promised Maddie a big white wedding cake, like was all the rage these days. But that was because he didn't want his bride to get any ideas about serving gingerbread cookies instead.

"I'm happy for Maddie," Grace said, not realizing until the words were out how melancholy they sounded.

"But you're feeling a little sorry for yourself."

It was hard hearing her father say those words out loud. "Yes," she finally whispered.

"That handsome Scotsman wouldn't have anything

to do with it, would he?" Her father raised his glass of lemonade and eyed her carefully over the rim.

"Why—why would he have any part in this?"

Pa smiled and shook his head, then looked down into his lap as if it held all the answers. "A blind man could see what was going on between the two of you."

Grace sighed and shook her head. "There's nothing to see."

He sat up a little straighter in his seat. "It may have been a long time ago, but I remember what love looks like."

"Like it matters."

"What's that mean?"

"He lives in New York, and my place is here."

Her father tapped one hand against his chin in a thoughtful gesture. "That may well be," he said. "Yesterday. But today, I think things are a bit different."

Different didn't even begin to describe it. "But—" She changed her mind about her protests and shook her head instead.

"Where is he now?"

"At the house, I suppose."

"Harlan and Maddie's house?"

Grace nodded. "Where else would he be?"

Pa shook his head. "He can't stay there. The house isn't even finished yet."

"Well he is."

"You need to go get him."

"Go get him?" Grace's heart tripped over itself. She

couldn't go get him. "Why?"

"So he can stay here, of course."

Stay here?

"Go on now."

Her father couldn't be serious. But he looked serious enough.

Grace reluctantly stood and ran her hands over her skirt. She would never disobey her father. But her heart tumbled in her chest. With anticipation. With excitement. With dread. She cast one last look at her father, trying to make sure he really meant what he said, but he had gone back to his paper.

She let herself out the back way, held up her skirts, and made her way across the field where she had walked with Ian just a short while ago. Except they had walked around the field, not through the multitude of flowers. She should've changed clothes before she left, but she didn't think about her skirts dragging through the plants until she got in the middle of the meadow. She hiked up her skirts a little more and continued on. Best get this over with quickly.

The house that Harlan was building fell somewhere in between modest and ostentatious. A large wraparound porch stretched across the front, disappearing around either side. Garret windows pushed through the roof, their real glass panes twinkling in the sun. Grace dashed up the steps and had only just gotten to the door when it opened.

"Oh!" she exclaimed.

Ian stood framed in the doorway, looking even more handsome than he had at the wedding. He had not forgotten to change clothes, and now wore workaday trousers and a shirt with suspenders, like any of the men in Calico Falls.

That made her both sad and anxious. Sad because she missed the kilt and anxious because she didn't need him looking like any of the men that surrounded her. He was unattainable. Off limits. And despite the feelings of head-over-heels love she experienced the first time her eyes met his, he was not part of God's plan for her.

"Grace." His voice was low and husky.

"Pa sent me. He said you couldn't stay here tonight. The house isn't even done. You'll have to come sleep with me."

Heat filled Grace's face, and she didn't need a mirror to know she had turned an unbecoming shade of red. She was burning up. "I mean, us."

One of Ian's rusty brows shot toward his hairline.

"I mean, stay at our house." She was only making this worse. "I mean you need a decent place to stay—this house isn't done. When Maddie and Harlan get back, they're staying with us. You can't stay here."

He looked pointedly toward her feet then cleared his throat.

Grace glanced down. She still had her skirts hiked

up almost to her knees. Scandalous. What had she been thinking? She dropped her skirts and smoothed her hands over them as if somehow to take away the fact that she flashed him more than just her ankles. "Sorry," she murmured. "This situation seems to have brought out the worst in me."

"Think nothing of it."

She shifted from one foot to the other, waiting for him. He cleared his throat again. "I'll be fine here."

Grace shook her head. "Pa insisted."

Ian seemed to mull it over for a few moments then he gave a quick nod. "Let me get my things."

Ian felt a little like a puppy dog following behind his master, as he walked behind Grace all the way back to the preacher's house. He'd never seen a woman move so fast, like her feet were on fire. It was as if she wanted to spend as little time with him as possible.

As badly as he wanted to spend every waking moment with her, those moments were limited. Still, he loved the way she blushed when she said that he was to come sleep with her, an innocent and honest mistake, but one he enjoyed all the same.

"Wait up," he called, hurrying after her. Somehow his thoughts had taken over and stilled his steps. Now she was yards ahead of him instead of merely feet.

Whether she didn't hear him or she was outright ignoring him, he didn't know. But he quickened his pace again and caught her. He wrapped his hand around her arm and stopped her in her tracks.

"Why are you walking so fast? Is there a fire? Or something you didn't tell me about?"

She shook her head. "It's better this way, don't you think?"

"What way? Sprinting across a meadow?"

"No, not being alone together."

"I think it's too late for that." Ian chuckled.

She whirled on him. "It's not funny!" She spun back around and marched toward home again.

He headed after her, this time catching her in three easy strides. "It's hysterical."

"I beg to differ." She sniffed and raised her chin to a haughty angle.

"What happened to God playing tricks on us? I'm sure He's laughing right about now."

She shook her head. "God has more important things to do than mess with our meager lives."

"Does He have more important things than providing us with love and companionship?"

"I'm not destined to have those things."

"Who told you that?"

"It's something I know. Something I've always known. My mother died when I was five. Since then I've been at my father's side, helping him with the church. That is my calling."

His humor dried up faster than a rain puddle in July. "I have a calling, too."

She seemed to wilt right before his eyes. Her chin dropped and her jade-green eyes swam with tears. "What do we do?"

"First thing is not to cry." He couldn't stand to see a woman's tears, especially when there was nothing on earth he could do to stop them. "And the next is to do what we can."

"I don't understand."

He heaved a sigh. "We can only do what we can do."

"Ian, stop talking in riddles." She closed her eyes and twin tears spilled down her cheeks.

"We can only make the best of the situation. We can only spend a little time together and that's all."

"I would love to spend time with you, but—"

"I know." She didn't have to finish. Spending time together would only make the longing worse. "But the time we will spend together, that's all there is. Are you willing to accept that?"

She nodded.

What choice did they have? "Me, too."

Her jade green eyes opened once again, this time clear with understanding. "And come Tuesday, you'll leave."

He nodded.

"Until then?"

"We can be friends. We can do that, right? Just enjoy what time we have."

"And then it's gone."

He swallowed the lump in his throat. "Yes."

She sent a trembling smile his way. "If that's all we have, then we need to take it."

"So we're agreed."

She nodded.

He took her arm in his hand and together they walked across the field, back to the white clapboard house at the edge of town.

The feel of her walking beside him, the building of love, and the knowledge this would be all they could have, stilled his words in his throat. Silently he prayed.

Why now, Lord? Why did I have to find a woman like Grace now, when I can do nothing about it?

Chapter 3

Sunday morning dawned as perfect a day as the one before it. Grace had enjoyed eating dinner with Ian. Of course her father and Prissy were there as well, but it was much easier to relax and enjoy herself when she wasn't looking to the future, but living in the moment as it were. Afterwards, her father had his pipe in the parlor while Grace played church hymns on the piano. All in all, it had been a good evening. She even managed to sleep, knowing that Ian was just down the hall and Maddie wasn't.

"We walk to church," Easton explained. After breakfast the four of them set off down the packed-dirt road that led to Calico Falls and the little white church at the end of the lane.

They got there early as usual, and Grace took the

position standing next to her father greeting his flock as they arrived.

This was her job, her calling, as she had told Ian. Her place in the world. She caught him looking at her as she hugged the Widow Barnes and could tell from the sad mist in his eyes that he understood.

But she got to sit next to him when her father took to the pulpit.

She loved to hear him preach, and today was no exception.

"It's simple to understand God's will for your life. All you have to do is answer three simple questions."

Funny, but her father looked straight at her when he said the words.

"Is it in the Bible?" He turned just enough to fix his gaze on Ian. "Is this the desire of your heart? And is there a need?" He turned back to look at Grace. "If you can answer no to any of these, then it may not be God's plan for you." Gaze back on Ian.

Then he turned to his Bible. "The book of Jeremiah tells us in Chapter twenty-nine, verses eleven through thirteen. 'For I know the thoughts that I think toward you, saith the Lord, thoughts of peace, and not of evil, to give you an expected end. Then shall ye call upon me, and ye shall go and pray unto me, and I will hearken unto you. And ye shall seek me, and find me, when ye shall search for me with all your heart.'"

Pray, that's what she needed to do. But for what? For patience? Understanding? None of those would change the facts: her life was in Calico Falls and Ian's was in New York. No amount of prayer could change that.

There had been many a sermon Ian had listened to that seemed as if the preacher was speaking straight to him, but there was no mistaking that Easton Sinclair had singled him out for his subject today. God's will and knowing what God wants from your life. Yesterday morning he thought he knew, but today, he wasn't so sure.

All morning Grace hugged parishioners and greeted everyone as they came to worship. She was the perfect preacher's daughter, Ian had thought as she smiled and shook hands. The congregation loved her as well, chatting with her about everything from apple pie recipes to how beautiful the wedding had been. He just stood to one side and watched, just as he was watching now, as she and her father said their farewells.

The perfect preacher's daughter would make the perfect preacher's wife, that little voice inside him whispered.

Why now, Lord? Of all the people in the world he could fall for, why her? It was true what they said, the good Lord did work in mysterious ways, but for the life of him, he couldn't figure out why God would want him to fall for someone he couldn't have.

But the Lord only answered with one word Ian seemed to hear from Him all too often. *"Patience."*

Ian continued to watch as they turned down several offers for a Sunday meal, reminding everyone that they had company. And soon they were walking back to the pastor's house.

After a dinner of wedding leftovers, Easton suggested they all go for a walk.

Everyone agreed. After all, it was a beautiful day and considering all the food he had eaten during the last two days, Ian could use a bit of exercise.

Together the four of them, he, Easton, Grace, and Prissy, headed across the field of wildflowers.

"Is this a good idea?" Grace asked. She and Ian had dropped behind her father and Prissy, allowing the other couple to move farther ahead.

"What? Going for a walk?"

"No, spending this much time together."

"I thought we had settled this. We're friends right?"

She nodded, but he noticed she hesitated before agreeing.

"Friends can go on a walk."

"You're right, of course."

He was reaching for reasons, but she had agreed to spend time with him and that's all that mattered.

He wanted to grab her hand so badly, entwine their fingers, but that wasn't friend behavior, so he had to settle for her simply walking at his side.

"The flowers are beautiful." Grace trailed her fingers along the higher petals and Ian remembered her saying this very field was where Maddie's wedding bouquet had been picked.

He stopped, the urge to gather Grace her own flowers taking hold. He picked as many different colors as he could, wishing he had a ribbon to tie them all together for her.

She turned as if she had only then realized he wasn't by her side.

"For you." He used a long stem to tie the bundle together and presented them to her.

Her smile let him know just how much he would miss her when he left. She held the flowers close to her face, breathing in the sweet scent. "Thank you," she murmured. But her joy at the simple gift was more than enough thanks.

They started to walk again. Up ahead of them, Easton had stopped and picked a single wild daisy and presented it to Prissy. She curtsied and tucked the flower behind her ear.

"Are they..." Ian nodded toward the couple, leaving the rest of his sentence unsaid. It wasn't really his business, but it was a strange relationship to be sure.

Grace shrugged, and he let the matter drop. It was too beautiful of a day for speculations.

Two more steps and Ian watched as Easton crumpled into a heap.

Grace stifled back a scream as her father fell. She hiked up her skirts and raced to his side.

"I'm all right. I'm all right." Her father chuckled embarrassingly and pushed to his feet. He brushed himself off as he continued to laugh.

But his good-natured grin turned to a grimace when he put weight on his right foot. He nearly crumpled to the ground once again, but managed to catch himself before he actually fell.

"Oh dear." Prissy grabbed one of his arms while Grace caught the other and together, with Ian bracing him from behind, they managed to get him safely back to the house.

"What happened?" Grace asked once they had Pa in his favorite chair, his right foot propped up on a small, cushioned stool.

"Stepped in a hole, I guess."

"Let me take a look, sir."

Grace stepped aside as Ian came forward. He gently pulled up her father's pant leg while she peeked over his shoulder.

"What is it?" she asked.

"I don't know. I'm not exactly a doctor."

"I'll get a cold rag and some ice," Prissy said and hustled toward the kitchen.

"I'll be fine," her pa blustered, pushing his pant leg back in place. "No sense flashing my ankles all over creation."

Grace straightened, and Ian did the same. He caught her eye and she was instantly taken back to the day before, standing on the porch of her sister's new house with her skirts up to her knees.

Her face filled with fire at the light in his eyes, a light that said he was thinking the same thing.

She turned away before she completely burned up, thankful then that Prissy bustled back into the room, carrying a large pan and a hunk of ice, half wrapped in a kitchen towel.

"Move back," she admonished, stirring Grace to action.

She stepped out of the way, and Ian followed suit.

"No sense in you young folks hanging around. Go on out and finish your walk."

"Yes, Pa."

Together they stepped from the room, but the desire to laze about in the bright summer sun was replaced with concern for her father.

"I hope it's nothing serious," she said.

From the tight set of Ian's mouth, she couldn't tell how he felt about the matter. Or maybe he was frowning over her scandalous exhibit yesterday. Surely he knew that she didn't go about like that all the time. Or even often.

"It's hard to say," Ian finally said, his sky-blue eyes giving nothing away. "I guess we'll have to wait and see how he is tomorrow."

But Monday dawned with Easton still unable to walk. Frankly, Ian was concerned. There didn't appear to be anything wrong with Easton's ankle. But Ian wasn't a doctor, he was a pastor. How was a man of God supposed to know about invisible injuries?

They ate breakfast, each lost in their own concerns about Easton's mysterious injury. Afterward, they helped him to the parlor, where he took up his spot in the same place as the night before, pipe at the ready, newspaper at hand, foot on the stool, and frown on his face.

"I'll be fine, I tell you." He shot his oldest daughter a pointed look that brooked no argument.

Ian had a feeling the spirited Maddie would have fought her father over the matter, but Grace was more reserved. He could practically see her calming herself, biding her time to make the most of her arguments.

"Very well," she said, but Ian knew the matter was far from over. "I guess I'll get Maddie and Harlan's room ready for their return." She nodded toward Ian as if to excuse herself.

Helplessly he watched her head for the parlor door. He wished he had some reason, any excuse to call her back and have her spend the day with him.

"Oh, I almost forgot."

Ian turned to find Easton's eyes sparkling with something akin to mischief. He wasn't sure the look could be trusted, but it was there, all the same.

Grace turned as well. "Yes, Pa?"

"I almost forgot that Tom Daniels has been sick. His neighbor asked for me to go out there today and pray with the family. And now. . ." He waved a vague hand toward his injured foot. Then he snapped his fingers, the action too deliberate to be anything but planned. "I know. How 'bout the two of you go out there in my stead." It wasn't quite a question.

"But Maddie's room. . ." Grace trailed off as Easton shook his head.

"Prissy can handle that."

"And who will take care of you?" She winced as she said the words, as if she could hear how weak they sounded before they even left her lips.

"Bah, I'm fine, I tell you. I have my pipe and the paper." He patted his Bible sitting on the table next to him. "When I get done with that, then I can work on my next sermon."

Ian could almost see Grace crumble. She really was a delightful soul, willing to help. So beautiful. And so out of his reach. *You've already decided this, McGruer. Get your head right and your priorities straight.* Tomorrow morning he would be on his way back to Albany. And that was that.

But today he was riding out to the Daniels' farm to pray over a sick man. How could he say no to that?

"Of course," Grace said in that elegant way of hers. "I'll hitch up the wagon."

Ian stepped forward. "Allow me."

A stricken look crossed her face, but it vanished almost as fast as it had appeared. She nodded. "Let me get my Bible, and I'll meet you out front."

The last thing—the very last thing—she wanted was to be riding out to the Daniels' farm with Ian McGruer. But there she was, sitting next to him, doing her best not to let their shoulders accidently touch as they swayed along.

He felt the same. She could tell. He was leaning so far left he was almost falling out of the wagon as they ambled down the country lane.

So much for wedding bouquets determining who was getting married next. Just another fantasy built to break girls' hearts when it didn't come true. Thank heavens she didn't let her hopes get too high. Still. . .

The bouquet of wildflowers Ian had presented her worked its way into her thoughts. So sweet and beautiful. Yet, she had dropped them when her father had fallen. It was for the best. That was one less thing she needed:

another bouquet with too much meaning behind it and a dead end ahead.

And the flower her father had given Prissy. They might be all God's children, but where could a romance between the preacher and his dark-skinned housekeeper lead?

They were almost to the farm when Ian cleared his throat, rupturing the silence and breaching her thoughts. "Your father is acting sort of strangely, yes?"

"You mean with Prissy?"

He shook his head, and Grace immediately regretted letting her thoughts go so easily. "His ankle."

"It's very unfortunate," she said. "I'm glad he didn't get hurt before the wedding. Maddie would have been crushed if he couldn't have stood up long enough to marry them."

Ian cleared his throat again. "So you don't think he's faking?" His voice dipped on the last word, so low she almost didn't hear it.

"No." She shook her head, pushing away any doubts that had been creeping in. "He can't be faking. My father is a good Christian man. Why would he lie about something like hurting his ankle? Unless. . ." She turned to look at Ian. Was her father trying to push her toward Ian? Pa had certainly managed to get them together in the wagon fast enough. Why would her father want to do that? So she would fall completely in love with the young preacher and move away and be heartbroken for having to leave her family? She could barely stand it now that Maddie was gone. Is that what her father wanted?

The look in Ian's eyes said he understood and was thinking the same thing as she.

But it was just as likely they could both be wrong about her father's injury. It was a small hope, but one she would cling to all the same.

Chapter 4

The Daniels' farm was in worse shape than Grace had imagined. Weeds grew in the garden among the ripening fruits and vegetables, and she could see as soon as they pulled up that the barn needed tending.

Ian set the brake and jumped to the ground. He came round to her side and lifted her down before she could protest. His touch on her waist as he guided her was chaste and necessary, but it still made her wonder about things that could never be.

She pushed those thoughts aside and concentrated on the farm.

"Looks pretty run down," he commented. "How long has Daniels been sick?"

"A couple of weeks." She thought back. "Maybe more."

How had they slipped through their thoughts? Her father was dutiful about keeping up with his parishioners.

The wedding, Grace realized, and said a quick prayer of forgiveness for letting her personal life get in the way of her duty to church and community.

"Looks like there's a good bit more to do here than pray."

The door to the house swung open, and a young boy stepped out into the yard. He shifted the slop bucket to one hand and tried to shut the door behind him. But his efforts stilled when he saw them standing there.

"Ma? There's people out here."

Grace searched her brain to remember the boy's name. "Hi, Gordon. Do you remember me? I'm Grace, the preacher's daughter."

His eyes lit with recognition then settled warily on Ian.

"This is my friend," she said. "His name is Mr. McGruer, and he's a preacher, too."

"Gordon, why are you standing here with the door op—" The lady of the house came to a quick stop when she caught sight of her guests. She flung the dishtowel she had been using to dry her hands across one shoulder, her fingers immediately flying to her hair.

Frazzled. That was the best word Grace could think of to describe the woman. Her shoulders slumped, her dress was dirtied, and dark circles lined her weary eyes. Tired, worn, and on her last leg. It seemed Grace had another request for forgiveness to make.

"Mrs. Daniels, I'm so sorry it's taken me so long to come check on you. We missed you at church yesterday."

The woman flashed a quick smile toward them and urged Gordon toward the pig pen. "Go on now, son. The beasts are waiting."

The boy did as he was told, leaving the adults standing at the door.

"This is my friend, Ian McGruer," Grace continued, all too aware of the hand Ian had placed at the small of her back. Was he even aware that he was touching her?

"It's nice to meet you," he said.

Mrs. Daniels stood a little straighter then dipped in a small curtsey toward the man. Her smile was wide and a few of the lines left her face. Grace knew all too well the smile he had bestowed on the lady. "Won't you come in?" She stood to the side to allow them entrance into the cluttered house. "I apologize for the mess. Tom has been sick a while and well, it's hard for me and Gordon to keep up with everything ourselves. Can I make you some coffee or tea?"

Grace shook her head. "Thank you, though. The pastor fell yesterday and is laid up with a twisted ankle." At least that's what she thought was wrong. "He asked us to come out and pray over Mr. Daniels."

But it was obvious more than prayer was needed to help this household. Dishes were stacked near the washtub. The floor needed a good sweeping and, for the most part, the little house sagged under the weeks of neglect.

Tears welled in Mrs. Daniels's eyes, but she blinked them back, managing to hold on to what was left of her dignity and pride. "Please, sit for a spell." She collapsed into one of the wobbly chairs surrounding the small wooden table and gestured for them to do the same.

Grace eased into a chair and laid her hand on top of one of Mrs. Daniels's. Vaguely aware of Ian sitting across from her, she focused her attention on the weary lady in front of her. "Would you like for us to pray for you as well, Mrs. Daniels?"

"Esther," she corrected with a weak smile.

Grace returned the smile and reached for Ian's hand. Together the three of them prayed for health, strength, and healing.

For the remainder of the afternoon, Ian and Grace worked beside Gordon and Esther doing more than just praying. He mucked stalls, cleaned stables, weeded the garden, and groomed horses until he was certain he wouldn't be able to move come the morning.

But he had never spent a more satisfying day. He had prayed, worked the land, and prayed some more. And all with the most beautiful woman he had ever known.

He had watched Grace with Esther and Gordon Daniels. She had laughed with them, empathized with them, and then helped them get back on their feet.

She had prayed with Tom Daniels, swept floors, and didn't think twice about washing clothes in what had to be one of her best Sunday dresses. Never before had he met a woman like her. She was all he could hope for in a life partner, but she was not for him. The longer he watched her, the more apparent it became that she belonged here with this country church and the people who needed their pastor in so many different ways than those who lived in the big cities.

Suddenly he wanted to be a part of that life, to muck stalls and milk cows and pray for the infirm, and the healthy who were affected by a loved one's illness, all in the same day. But he had made his promise to the First Church of Albany.

Just because he wanted it to be so didn't mean it could truly be that way. God had plans for them both; despite the overwhelming feelings he had for Grace Sinclair.

He helped her into the wagon and after waving good-bye to the very grateful Esther and Gordon, the two of them set off for home.

"Thank you," she said quietly.

"For what?"

"Helping the Daniels."

"I'm a pastor. It's my job to help those in need."

"Praying and counseling. But you didn't have to do all the farm work. I could tell that you aren't used to such chores."

He chuckled. "That's true. I haven't worked on a farm in many years. Since my family came over to America."

"How old were you then?"

"Eight."

She tried to imagine him then, scrawny and gangly, rusty hair a bit shaggy around the ears, blue eyes with the innocent light only the youth can hold. "But you did before that?"

"Yes. In Scotland; my family had a small farm, sheep and such."

"I bet that was beautiful."

"It was very beautiful. In fact, Arkansas reminds me a lot of East Lothian. Oh, not the weather. But the fields and the hills, the green grass."

Grace tried to imagine, but Scotland seemed so exotic compared to workaday Arkansas. She couldn't imagine anything the two places had in common, save the man who sat next to her. "Do you still have family there? In East Lothian?"

"My grandparents stayed. As did most of the family. I've got a herd of aunts and uncles still living there, scores of cousins."

"Do you miss them?"

He shrugged. "It's been almost twenty years. I'm from New York now."

Grace fell quiet, allowing his words to wash over her. His life was in New York as much as hers was in Calico Falls, but what she wouldn't give for a common place for the two of them, somewhere in between where they could be together and let their love grow.

"Maddie!" Grace rushed down the steps and greeted her sister with open arms. She may have only been gone for a couple of days, but it had been a very eventful weekend and she needed to connect with her sister again.

Maddie returned her hug, her smile wide and eyes sparkling.

That was what love did to a woman, made her confident and beautiful. Suddenly Grace was more envious of Maddie than she had been their entire lives.

"Come in, come in," Prissy called from the door, waving the returning couple inside. "Supper's almost on the table."

They all washed up and gathered round. Even Pa managed to hobble his way to the table. His limp looked a little different, though Grace couldn't tell if it was better or worse. But, she decided, if he wasn't back to himself in the morning, she would go fetch the doctor.

Their meal was a bright affair. Grace loved listening to Maddie talk about their time in the city, staying in the hotel, and having people bring them food to their room. The thought of lounging about and enjoying the company of the one she loved sounded so sweet; it almost brought tears to her eyes. She had never really thought about it before, that she would have such a relationship with another. Oh, maybe when she had been a young girl, but as an adult, the thought was never allowed to cross her mind. But now that it had. . .

She cast a look at Ian. He was seated next to her, listening as quietly and intently as she had been. But when her gaze fell upon him, he turned as if the touch had been physical. His eyes met hers and she knew their thoughts were the same.

She gave him a sad smile then looked away.

"So," Maddie started, her bright green gaze darting from Grace to Ian then back again. "Anything interesting happen while we were away?" Maddie's eyes settled on Grace, and suddenly she felt like a beetle pinned to a board in a little boy's bug collection.

"Pa fell and twisted his ankle." What else could she say?

"Uh-huh." Maddie's attention was unwavering.

"Oh, I'm fine," he started, then quickly followed it with, "Or I will be. In a day or two. . .maybe a week. But it's okay since I have Ian here to help with the duties."

"Duties?" Harlan looked from Ian to Pa, then he too

turned his attention to Grace.

She squirmed in her seat. "Ian and I went out to visit the Daniels' farm. Tom has been sick. His poor wife and son have been working their fingers to the bone trying to keep up."

Maddie smiled as if Grace had confessed that Ian had taken her out in the wagon and kissed her silly. "Really? That is interesting."

Grace frowned. "It is nothing of the sort. It's downright sad."

Maddie forked up a large bite of mashed potatoes. "Mmm-hmmm," she said, the food keeping her from any further answer.

"So as long as Ian stays here until I get back on my feet." Her father chuckled. "Both of them," he clarified, "I think everything will be just fine."

"I thought you were leaving tomorrow." Harlan raised his brows at his friend.

Ian shrugged. "I can't really leave his church in need."

"What about your church?" Harlan asked.

"I'm just one of three pastors. They'll get along fine without me for a day or two."

"Maybe a week," her pa interjected.

"Or a week," Ian conceded.

Grace wasn't sure if she should be happy Ian was staying a few more days or feeling sorry for herself, that she would have more days to fight these feelings she carried for him.

She caught Ian's gaze. Filled with remorse, it brought a lump to her throat. "I'm sorry," she mouthed to him.

He pressed his lips together and gave a small nod. For a moment she was lost in the bottomless blue of his eyes.

Then a nudge under the table.

Maddie grinned at her in a knowing way that sent alarm bells clanging in her head.

Harlan frowned, but Grace couldn't tell if he was upset or concerned.

At the head of the table, Pa's grin was wider than Maddie's. Grace knew then, if the two of them had anything to say about it, Ian would never make it back to New York. The thought was thrilling and infuriating all at the same time.

Chapter 5

After supper, Maddie and Harlan decided to walk over to the house and look around before it got dark.

They invited Grace and Ian, but they turned them down so quickly the couple looked as if they had been slapped.

Pa limped his way to the parlor and set himself up with his pipe while Prissy took care of the supper dishes.

"Do you want to go for a walk?" Ian asked, as Grace tried to decide what to do with the rest of her evening.

"I didn't think you wanted to go for a walk." He had told Harlan no quickly enough.

"It's not that I don't want to walk."

"You're not tired after all that work you did today?" she asked.

"Not that tired."

Grace gave a small nod. "Do you think it's a good idea? I mean, I thought we weren't going to spend any more time alone."

"We were alone all afternoon, and we managed to get through that just fine."

True, but it had taken all of her self-discipline to endure, and she just didn't have much left where he was concerned. Plus, she wanted to walk with him. If only for one last time. "All right, then. Yes, I'll walk with you."

They headed down the road toward town. Grace was sure Ian started in that direction to keep them well away from Maddie and Harlan's blatant meddling.

She wanted him to reach out and hold her hand, make some sort of contact, but they merely ambled along, side by side, neither one touching.

It's better this way. She knew that in her head, but her heart had started wanting more than her brain knew was right. Could two people in love with each other remain friends? It was the question of the ages.

"Is it mad?" she finally asked. "These feelings we have for each other?"

He shook his head. "I've asked myself that same thing a hundred times since I met you."

"And have you answered yourself, yet?" Grace tried to make light, but her voice held a weary edge.

"I just know what I know." His cryptic words fell

between them, confusing her all the more.

"And what is that?"

"My grandmother always said that God made someone special for each of us. When we meet that person we'll know it. My someone is you. Every day I spend with you confirms it time and again."

Grace stopped, shaking her head as she tried to make sense of a love that was beyond reason. "It can't be. I can't leave here."

"I know." He took her hands into his own and squeezed her fingers. His touch was like a piece of heaven on earth, the home she had always dreamed of, the one true love she had always wanted. "That's what makes this so confusing."

"I've spent my entire life trying to live by what God wants from me. All this time I thought I knew what that was."

He nodded and she knew she didn't have to continue. He felt the same as she. *Why now, Lord? Why now?*

"I think your father is trying to get us together."

"But that would mean I'd have to leave." A wife's place was with her husband. It would be her responsibility to follow Ian. Who would help her father? Is that what he wanted for her?

"And that would make you unhappy."

She nodded. Being married to Ian would be the most wonderful thing in the world, but being away from her family just didn't seem right. Was she looking at this all wrong? Was she being unreasonable? She couldn't imagine life outside of Calico Falls. If that's what God intended for her, shouldn't she at least be able to picture it in her head?

But if Ian wasn't the one God intended for her, why did she feel the way she did?

"If things could be different," he started, "and you didn't have to leave here. . . ?"

"Then there would be no question." She blushed. She was being so very forward, but there was something different about Ian McGruer. He wasn't like any man she had ever met. "If things could be different, would you. . . ?"

He nodded.

He wanted to kiss her; she could see it in his eyes. Yet what good would it do? It would only serve to break both their hearts. Right now they were a little bruised, but they would recover.

He released her hands and shoved his into his pockets as if he didn't trust them to be free.

"Is this a test?" she finally asked. "Like God gave to Abraham? Is he testing my faith? Your faith?"

Ian took her elbow and they headed back to the house. "I wish I knew. Oh, how I wish I knew."

"Grace?" Maddie's whisper floated across the darkness. The door to Grace's room swung gently inward as her sister filled the soft light filtering in from the hall. "Are you awake?"

"Maddie?"

Her sister flew across the room and jumped into the bed next to Grace, snuggling under the covers like they did when they were little.

"What are you doing in here?"

"I wanted to talk to you." Maddie pulled the covers up under her arms and grinned at Grace.

"You're supposed to be with your husband," she groused, though secretly glad that her sister was there. Oh, how she was going to miss her when the house was finished.

"I know, but I wanted to see you. Ask you about Ian."

Grace's heart gave a hard pound at the mention of his name. "What about him?"

"Well, you love him, for one."

She sighed, unable to deny it. "It's that obvious?"

"Yes, but I'm in tune with love right now."

They lay there in the darkness, each one captured in her own thoughts until Grace asked, "Do you believe that God made someone out there for each of us?"

"Yes," Maddie said emphatically. "Do you?"

"I would like to believe so. But what happens when your someone turns out to be someone that isn't right for you?"

"What are you talking about? He's perfect for you."

Oh, how she wished that were true. "How can you say

that? He lives in New York."

"I had forgotten about *that*. Whatever was I thinking?" Maddie's tone dripped with sarcasm.

"Will you be serious? If I were to marry him, I would have to move away from Calico Falls."

"And?"

"Isn't that enough?"

Maddie pushed herself up onto her elbows, staring hard into Grace's eyes. The look was incredibly intense for whimsical Maddie, and Grace shifted uncomfortably under its weight. "Do you think that if Harlan needed to move away that I would hesitate for a moment? I mean, I would miss you terribly, but I love him."

"But Pa—"

"Doesn't need you as much as you think he does. Without you he would simply do something else."

The thought washed over her, almost stinging with the truth. Was she necessary to her father's church? Or was she only making his life easier? "Are you saying—?"

"I'm saying that if you love him, you shouldn't let anything stand in your way." She stopped, then her tone changed, lightened as she continued. "If you want I could go down and work out a deal with Old Lady Farley."

"Maddie, be serious."

"I am serious." But even in the dark bedroom, Grace could see her sister's eyes twinkling. "There's someone out there for you, Grace. Haven't we always dreamt of getting married and having babies? That dream will come true," she said.

But as confident as her sister sounded, Grace had her doubts.

Tuesday morning, Ian arose to another beautiful day in the Ozarks. Birds chirped, the wind rustled the green leaves, and the blue sky seemed to stretch on forever.

But when he made his way downstairs, he found Easton limping around and Grace frowning.

"I'm going to get Doc Williams," she said, ignoring her father's protests.

Ian glanced at Easton's ankle, still covered with his pant leg, then looked back to Grace. "Do you think it's that bad?"

She shrugged. "I don't know, but he's been limping around here for days and it's time to get the doctor."

"Just give me a couple more days," Easton grumped from his favorite chair.

Grace propped her hands on her hips, and Ian was convinced she had never looked prettier. "I have. Now it's time to get some professional help."

"Do you want me to walk with you?" Ian asked.

She shook her head. "I'll be fine."

But something in her tone said that she was distancing herself from him. As much as his heart ached at the thought, he knew it was for the best. They had tried ignoring their love. They had tried being friends. Neither had worked. Staying away from each other seemed to be the only solution they truly had.

Grace returned with the doctor in record time, sweeping into the parlor with the gray-haired man trailing in her wake.

Doc Williams had a thick moustache, wire-rimmed spectacles, and a string tie that bobbed when he talked. He folded up Easton's pant leg and gave his ankle a thorough examination. Everyone looked on with furrowed brows.

The doctor straightened and shook his head. "Well, Easton, I can't see anything wrong. But if it's hurting you, give it a couple days rest. Maybe stop by the office on Friday."

Easton pulled down his pant leg and crossed his arms as he surveyed his family. "See? Rest. That's what I need."

"And breakfast," Prissy called from the door to the kitchen. "Y'all come and get it."

Sitting around the table with Grace on one side and his best friend across from him, Ian wondered what it would be like to stay here in Calico Falls. Would every day be like this? Or was this just part of the visitors' trip and once he left things would go back to how they normally were? How was he even to know?

"Ian, would you mind going out to the Dursleys' this morning? Grace can go with you." Easton wiped his mouth on his napkin and looked at each of them in turn. Going out to another farm today was not the way to keep his distance from Grace, but how was he supposed to refuse?

"Harlan, why don't you go with Ian?" Grace asked. "Maddie and I have plans to start new dresses today."

"We do?" Maddie asked.

"Yes." Grace said, her jaw tight. "We do."

Ian felt the brush of her skirts against his calf, then watched as Maddie jumped across the table.

"Ow," she mouthed and he knew that Grace had kicked her sister in order to gain compliance.

"I can drive out there with you," Harlan said. "What's needed at the Dursleys'?"

"Mrs. Dursley's twins have been under the weather. They could use some prayers. And probably someone to play with for a while."

Harlan looked back to Ian. "Twins?" he mouthed.

Ian hid his smile. It looked like they were in for an eventful morning.

Eventful was not the best word to describe the morning at the Dursleys' farm. As far as Calico Falls went, the Dursleys had to have been one of the wealthiest families. Fences stretched for miles and livestock dotted the green fields in between. The two story house was well-kept, white-painted, and stood majestically to one side of the large red barn.

The Dursleys didn't need the same kind of care and attention that the Daniels had, but Ian enjoyed himself all the same. The twins were rough-housing, six-year-old boys just recovering from the chicken pox. Thankfully Ian and Harlan both had already had them. They spent the better part of the morning playing with the boys and generally getting them out of their mother's way for a while.

They ate lunch on the farm then headed back to the pastor's house. All the way there, Ian kept thinking about the church in Albany.

He had visited a couple of times before accepting the position. But now he wondered if he had been a little enchanted, maybe even overwhelmed with the thought that they wanted him, Ian McGruer, to be a pastor there. What in his humble training had made him worthy of such a large and prestigious church?

It was a big church and everyone dressed to the nines every Sunday. At the time, he had been impressed with all the fancy ties and hats, but thinking back, he realized now that a lot of the members were more concerned with how everyone looked instead of the Good Lord's message.

He needed to be fair, there were a lot of people who came for the Word, but it still wasn't like Calico Falls. The tiny town was filled with people who loved the Lord, their country, and their preacher. They pitched in when something needed to be done. They depended on each other in a way that he had never seen before.

And then there was the countryside. It was so beautiful and remarkably reminded him of his beloved Scotland. Of course it had been a great while since he had lived there, but just being near the lush green fields made him nostalgic for something he couldn't even name.

"Got something on your mind?" Harlan asked.

Ian stirred himself from his thoughts and faced his friend. He had been so lost in his own mind that he hadn't realized they were over halfway back to the parsonage. "You could say that."

"Do you need to talk about it?"

It was on the tip of his tongue to say yes, but he realized that talking about it wasn't going to change a thing. He needed to pray and pray hard that the Lord would give him the answer he needed.

Chapter 6

The next morning Pa came limping down the stairs. Grace bit back her sigh and her worry as she watched him slowly make his way across the parlor toward the kitchen. Something wasn't right.

"That's the wrong foot." She turned toward her father, feeling a bit surly as she pointed to him. Lack of sleep could do that to a person. And though she pleaded a headache and retired for the evening early in the afternoon, she hadn't slept much at all.

"What?" Pa stopped.

Ian and Harlan turned to stare at the two of them, and Grace immediately regretted her outburst.

"I—I mean, your limp," she tried again.

"Oh. Oh," her father said, continuing on his way. This

time both ankles were stiff, confusing Grace to whether she had been seeing things in his misplaced limp.

"I've hobbled around for so many days, both my legs are giving me fits now."

Surely lack of sleep was starting to play tricks on her mind. After all, she hadn't slept much since the wedding, not just the night before.

Ian and Harlan swung their gazes toward her, and she could do nothing but paste on a concerned look and try to cover up her shrill accusations. "Has anyone seen Maddie?"

"She's in the kitchen helping Prissy with breakfast," Harlan explained.

Grace nodded. "I'll just go check on everything then." She fled the room to the relative safety of the kitchen.

The interior was warm and smelled spicy and inviting, but Maddie shooed her out, stating that she had everything under control.

Grace had no reason to doubt her, as breakfast was on the table in record time. Soon the blessing had been offered and all that could be heard was the clink of silverware against the plates as everyone devoured their pancakes.

"These pancakes are delicious," Ian said, holding up a bite and examining it a moment before he stuffed it into his mouth.

Grace had to admit they were extra delicious this morning.

"It's a special recipe," Maddie explained, her green eyes sparkling.

"Bravo," Harlan said, shoveling in his own huge bite.

Soon everyone had finished their breakfast. Prissy waved the girls out of the kitchen.

"Grace?"

She closed her eyes at the sound of Ian's voice close behind her. She opened them again and turned to face him. "Yes?"

"Walk with me?"

She shook her head.

"Please," he pleaded. "It's important."

How could she refuse him a second time? "Okay."

Together they walked out into the field of wildflowers between the pastor's house and Harlan's. She had a feeling she knew what this was about. He was leaving. There would be no more speculation on what was the right thing to do.

Maddie's words rattled around inside Grace's head. Was she being unreasonable to think her father needed her? Should she take the chance on Ian and see what adventure might lie in her future? Was that what God wanted from her? Was that what He was trying to tell her?

She turned to Ian, these questions seeking a voice. All she had to do was tell him that she had changed her mind. She had thought about their situation, and if he would still have her, then she was willing to take the chance that God had something different in mind for her than she had originally thought.

But as she turned, he was there. Close. So very close. And then he was closer, cupping her face in his hands, his lips pressed to hers.

Grace's eyes fluttered closed and she swayed toward Ian, loving the feel of his fingers on her face, his lips on hers in the sweetest kiss she could have ever imagined. A kiss much, much better than the one Davey Miller gave her at the spring hoedown when they were thirteen. She had slapped him then, but she couldn't raise her hand against Ian. She was too far gone in love with him. She could admit that now. God really had intended him for her and her for him. Her place was at his side, wherever that might be.

He gave her one more little kiss then dropped to one knee.

She could only stare at him as he pulled a ring from his pocket. "Will you marry me?"

Her mother's ring sparkled in the palm of his hand. The ring her father had saved for her. "You've talked to my father?"

He shook his head.

Something wasn't right.

"How did you get that?" she asked.

"Maddie gave it to me."

Then she knew. Her heart sank in her chest and she bit

back her tears as she pulled Ian to his feet.

"What's the matter?" A confused frown pulled at his brow.

"I'm going to kill her," Grace stormed. She whirled on one heel, nearly tripping as the flowers tangled beneath her feet. Such a waste of good wildflowers. Heat filled her cheeks as she started back for the house.

"Killing is a sin," Ian said from somewhere behind her. Poor man. He had no idea what had been done to him. But she couldn't stop to explain now. He wouldn't believe her anyway.

"Then I'll just maim her." Grace marched into the house. "Maddie!" she called. Then louder, "Madeline Joy!"

Maddie pushed through the kitchen door to stand in the foyer, all wide-eyed and innocent. "Yes, sister?"

"What did you trade for this time?"

"I don't believe I know what you're referring to."

Grace opened her mouth to refute the claim, but closed it again as Ian came into the house.

He drew her gaze like a magnet draws metal and her heart broke all over again at the confusion and hurt on his face. "Grace, would you please tell me what's going on?"

"Yes, Grace," Maddie echoed.

Harlan cleared his throat but didn't say anything.

"It's a long story," she started, resisting the urge to pinch back the headache that was starting between her eyes.

"I have time."

She turned toward him then, wanting to explain but not knowing where to begin.

"I thought we had something special," Ian said.

"We do. We did. I mean it might have been special if Maddie hadn't..."

"I didn't do anything." Maddie held up both hands in surrender, though her eyes sparkled with that mischievous light Grace knew all too well.

"I don't understand," Ian said.

Harlan intervened, saving Grace from having to come up with a suitable answer. "Maybe we should all go into the parlor."

The last thing she wanted to do was drag this out, but knowing Maddie, she would hold on to her innocence for as long as possible.

For once Pa wasn't sitting there reading the paper or smoking his pipe. For that, Grace was grateful. She didn't need another witness to her sister's shenanigans.

"Now," Harlan started, "what's this all about?"

"I haven't the faintest idea," Maddie said demurely.

"Madeline! It's a sin to lie! You know very well what you did."

"Since you seem to be so confident as to my actions, why don't you share it with us all?"

Grace took a deep breath and reminded herself that she was a lady. No matter how badly she wanted to pull her sister's hair, like she did when they were younger, the coercion wouldn't make her admit her wrongdoings any more now than it had then. "You went down to Old Lady Farley's and got a love potion to put in the pancakes."

"I thought you didn't believe in such things. Isn't that you told me last Christmas?"

Grace faltered. "Well, maybe this time it really did work." Why else would Ian kiss her, like there was no tomorrow, and propose marriage after all they had discussed?

Maddie shot her husband a knowing look.

Harlan chuckled.

"Will someone tell me what's going on here?" Ian looked from one of them to the other. Grace couldn't blame the man. After everything he had been through. And he was just about to leave all the madness behind, when Maddie had to go and do something like this.

"Will you, darling?" Maddie asked, with a smile to her husband.

Harlan explained about the gingerbread cookies from the Christmas before. How Maddie, in her desperate attempts to get him to fall in love with her, had traded her second-best dress for a pouch of herbs guaranteed to make Harlan fall madly in love. "What she didn't know was that I was already crazy about her." He tapped one finger against her cheek. Maddie blushed and returned his smile. Somehow Grace felt like she had just witnessed an intimate moment between the two of them.

"Why haven't I heard this story before now?" Ian looked from Maddie to Harlan and back again, while Grace twisted her fingers in her lap. Why did everything have to turn out so complicated?

Harlan shrugged his big shoulders. "I don't know. It just never came up."

"And this love potion," Ian asked, "Did it work?"

Maddie smiled. "No, it was nothing more than nutmeg and vanilla."

"It did make for some tasty cookies," Harlan added, patting his trim waist in memory.

Grace squirmed in her seat as Ian turned and pinned her with a stare. "Do you really doubt me that much?"

She hadn't looked at it that way. "It's not that." She shook her head, gathering her thoughts. "The pancakes this morning—"

"Were tasty," Harlan interjected.

Maddie shushed him.

"You think they had a love potion in them and that's why I proposed?"

"I'm completely innocent," Maddie said.

This time Harlan shushed her.

"But the kiss. And the ring." That was no sort of explanation, but she hadn't the words. "It wasn't doubt," she finally added. She had jumped to conclusions and had forgotten to trust God.

Now, the man she loved most in the world, the man

God had created just for her, was slipping right through her fingers and she was helpless to stop it.

She closed her eyes. *Lord, if he's the one for me, help me. Help me find the words. Help me explain. Help me show him that I believe him. Show him how much I love him in return.*

"What's all the ruckus in here?" Pa strode into the room, taking in each of their expressions in turn. Grace could only imagine what he thought.

Wait. There was no limp in her father's steady gait. "You're healed?" she asked. Anything was better than dwelling on the prayer she sent up and the lack of answer she had received. *Sometimes God says no,* her father often said. Was this one of those times?

Pa pulled himself up a little straighter. "I, uh—I mean. . ." he blustered.

"You've been faking this whole time?" Grace asked.

"Well, I, I. . ."

Grace could almost see him coming up with excuses and then tossing them aside. "I needed to find a way to get Ian to stay," he finally said.

Now Grace was well and truly confused. "Can we go back and start at the beginning?"

"Like when I proposed?" Ian asked.

Grace pinched the bridge of her nose. "Ian, I'm—"

"Afraid to take a chance on me?"

She shook her head. "I had already decided that my place

is right by your side wherever your side happens to be."

"And if I decide to go back to New York and take over the church there?"

She took a steadying breath, but said without hesitation or heartbreak, "Then I'll go with you. If you'll have me."

"Have you? I'm never going to let you go." He fell to his knees then practically crawled across the floor to be in front of her. As if he was afraid that she would change her mind at any second, he slipped the ring onto her finger and pressed a sweet kiss to her fingertips. "I'll do anything and everything to keep you by my side."

Maddie squealed and clapped her hands as Grace basked in the glory of knowing that Ian loved her, and would always be there for her.

"What about the church?" Pa asked.

Ian released her hands, but didn't take his gaze from her. Grace felt the heat of that look as surely as his touch when he had trailed his fingers down her cheek. "What about the church?

"This has been sort of a test, you see."

All eyes swung to him. Pa shrugged. "I've been talking to the deacons. I'm retiring, and I want you to take over for me, Ian."

"Me?" he asked. "You're serious?"

"I am. The Lord has called me to do some work a little closer to my heart. Prissy and I are going to be traveling for a while. So, do you want my church or not?"

"More than anything." He stood and pulled Grace to her feet. She swayed toward him.

"Well, almost anything," he corrected, looking longingly into her eyes.

"Are you sure?" she whispered.

"That I want to marry you more than I want the church? Absolutely."

Grace shook her head. "About taking over a country church when you could have the big fancy cathedral in Albany."

"I prayed about it all night. God said this is where I need to be."

Maddie jumped to her feet. "You could have a fall wedding."

Autumn was beautiful in the Ozarks.

"Now, about this love potion," Ian asked. "Does it really work? Because I have this cousin..."

Grace laughed. "There might not be anything to Old Lady Farley's love herbs, but Maddie's wildflower wedding bouquet? I'm keeping that forever."

"As long as I'm there at your side," Ian said. "Right where I belong."

Amy Lillard is a 2013 Carol Award-winning author who loves reading romance novels from contemporary to Amish. She was born and raised in Mississippi, but now lives in Oklahoma with her husband and their teenage son. Amy can be reached at amylillard@hotmail.com and found on the web at www.amywritesromance.com.

For more 12 Brides of Summer titles, check out:

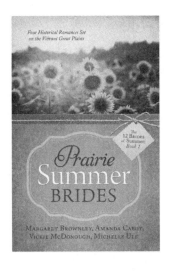

Prairie
Summer
BRIDES

Four enduring romances
from the prairie.

Old West
Summer
BRIDES

The old west sizzles with
four inspiring romances.

Available wherever Christian books are sold.